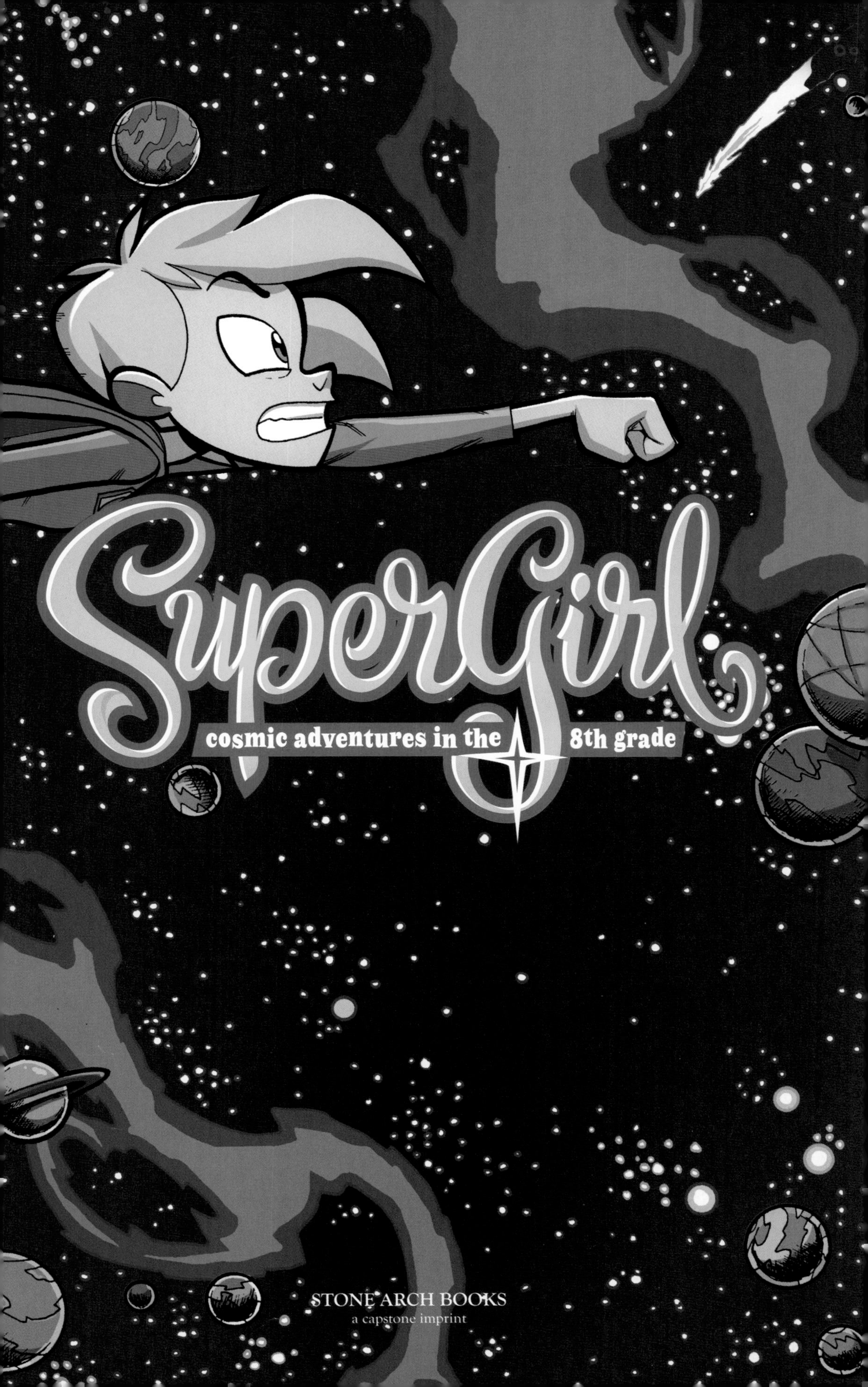
SuperGirl
cosmic adventures in the 8th grade
STONE ARCH BOOKS
a capstone imprint

STONE ARCH BOOKS™

Published in 2013
A Capstone Imprint
1710 Roe Crest Drive
North Mankato, MN 56003
www.capstonepub.com

Fallsburg Library
PO Box 730
South Fallsburg, NY 12779
845-436-6067

Originally published by DC Comics in the U.S. in single magazine form as Supergirl: Cosmic Adventures in the 8th Grade #6.

Copyright © 2013 DC Comics. All Rights Reserved.

DC Comics
1700 Broadway, New York, NY 10019
A Warner Bros. Entertainment Company

No part of this publication may be reproduced in whole or in part, or stored in a retrieval system, or transmitted in any form or by any means, electronic, mechanical, photocopying, recording, or otherwise, without written permission.

Cataloging-in-Publication Data is available at the Library of Congress website:

ISBN: 978-1-4342-6046-8 (library binding)

Summary: How will Supergirl ever wrap up all of the cosmic craziness that has developed since her arrival on Earth? Arch-frenemies, scheming faculty, an intergalactic orange kitty and a flying horse are just a few things that come her way in this final, action-packed issue!

STONE ARCH BOOKS
Ashley C. Andersen Zantop Publisher
Michael Dahl Editorial Director
Donald Lemke Editor
Heather Kindseth Creative Director
Brann Garvey Designer
Kathy McColley Production Specialist

DC COMICS
Jann Jones & Elisabeth V. Gehrlein Original U.S. Editors
Adam Schlagman U.S. Associate Editor
Simona Martore U.S. Assistant Editor

Printed in China by Nordica.
0413/CA21300442
032013 007226NORDF13

Super Girl
cosmic adventures in the 8th grade

OFF TO SAVE THE DAY!

LANDRY Q. WALKER
WRITER

ERIC JONES
ARTIST

JOEY MASON
COLORIST

PAT BROSSEAU
TRAVIS LANHAM
SAL CIPRIANO
LETTERERS

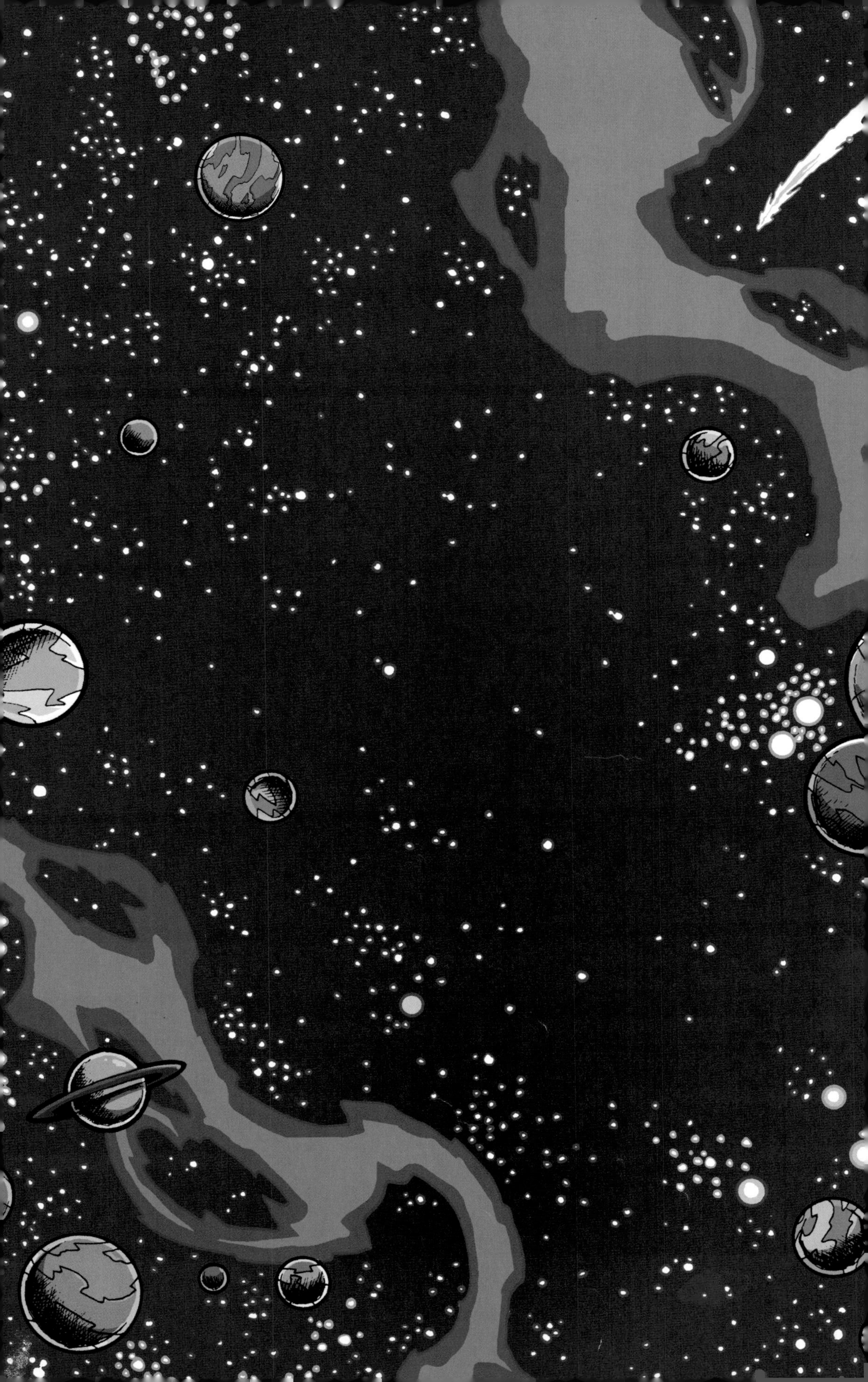

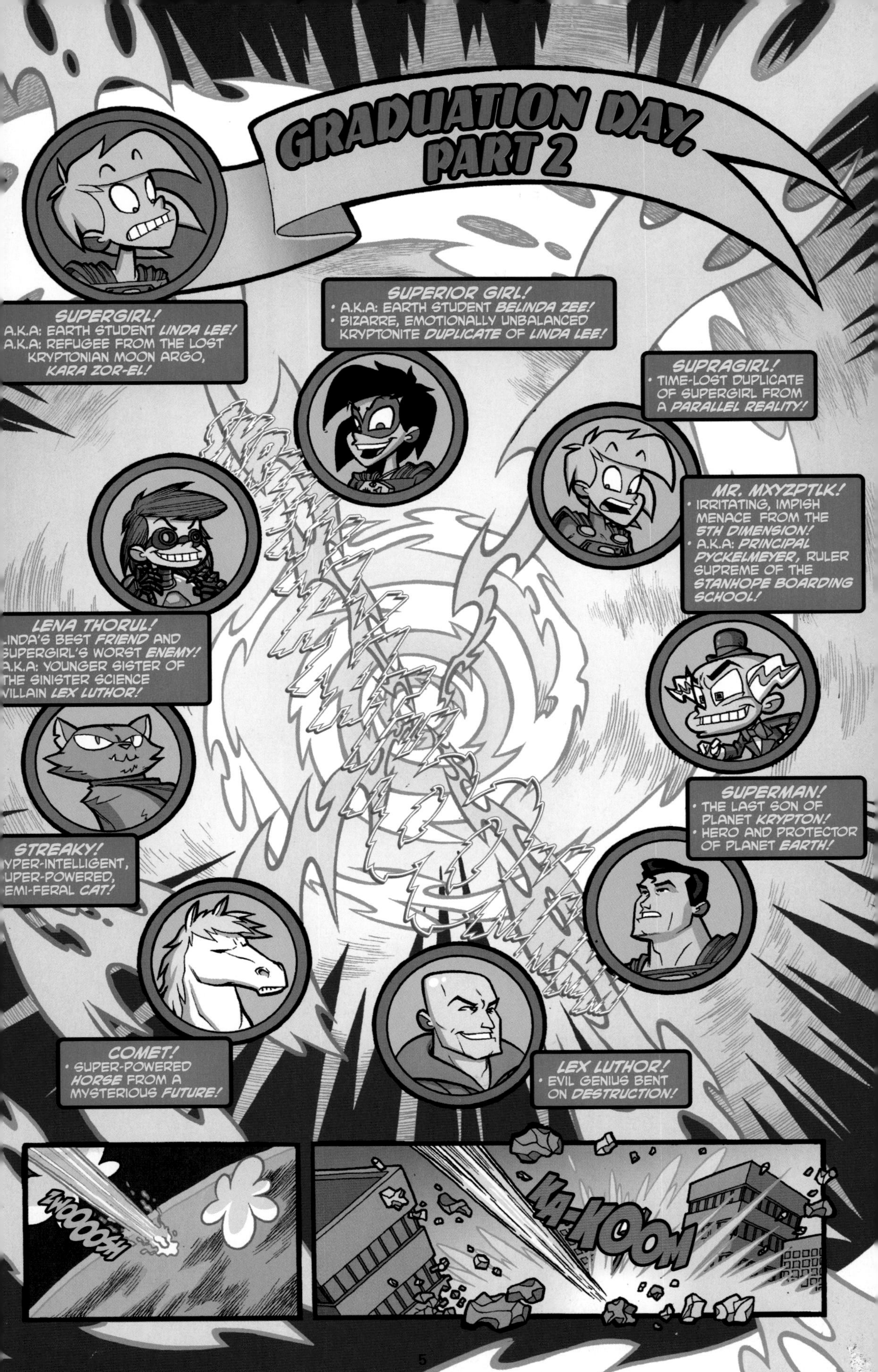
GRADUATION DAY, PART 2
SUPERGIRL!
A.K.A: EARTH STUDENT LINDA LEE!
A.K.A: REFUGEE FROM THE LOST KRYPTONIAN MOON ARGO, KARA ZOR-EL!
SUPERIOR GIRL!
• A.K.A: EARTH STUDENT BELINDA ZEE!
• BIZARRE, EMOTIONALLY UNBALANCED KRYPTONITE DUPLICATE OF LINDA LEE!
SUPRAGIRL!
• TIME-LOST DUPLICATE OF SUPERGIRL FROM A PARALLEL REALITY!
MR. MXYZPTLK!
• IRRITATING, IMPISH MENACE FROM THE 5TH DIMENSION!
• A.K.A: PRINCIPAL PYCKELMEYER, RULER SUPREME OF THE STANHOPE BOARDING SCHOOL!
LENA THORUL!
LINDA'S BEST FRIEND AND SUPERGIRL'S WORST ENEMY!
A.K.A: YOUNGER SISTER OF THE SINISTER SCIENCE VILLAIN LEX LUTHOR!
STREAKY!
HYPER-INTELLIGENT, SUPER-POWERED, SEMI-FERAL CAT!
SUPERMAN!
• THE LAST SON OF PLANET KRYPTON!
• HERO AND PROTECTOR OF PLANET EARTH!
COMET!
• SUPER-POWERED HORSE FROM A MYSTERIOUS FUTURE!
LEX LUTHOR!
• EVIL GENIUS BENT ON DESTRUCTION!
KA-KOOM

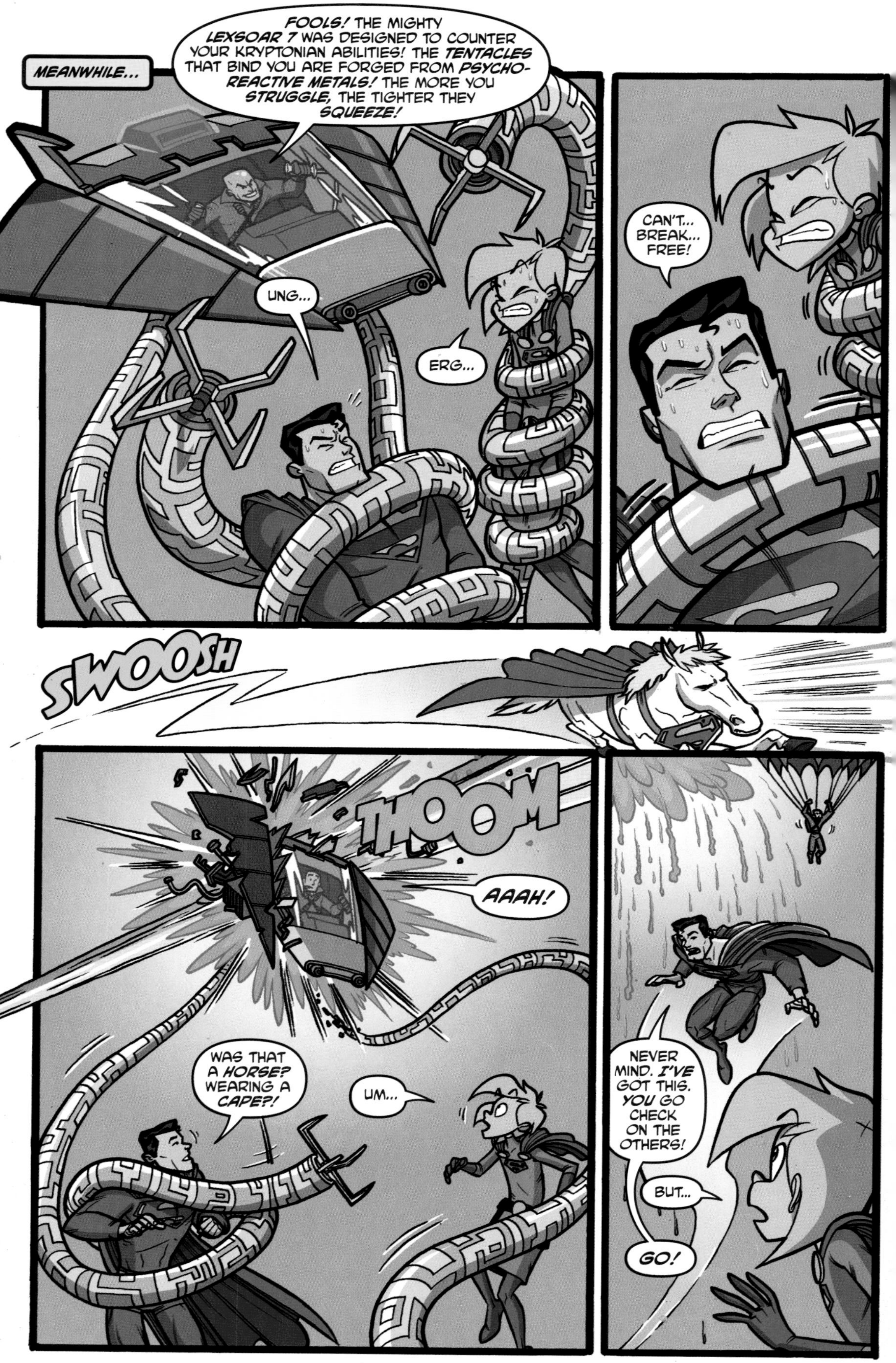
MEANWHILE...
FOOLS! THE MIGHTY LEXSOAR 7 WAS DESIGNED TO COUNTER YOUR KRYPTONIAN ABILITIES! THE TENTACLES THAT BIND YOU ARE FORGED FROM PSYCHO-REACTIVE METALS! THE MORE YOU STRUGGLE, THE TIGHTER THEY SQUEEZE!
UNG...
ERG...
CAN'T... BREAK... FREE!
SWOOSH
THOOM
AAAH!
WAS THAT A HORSE? WEARING A CAPE?!
UM...
NEVER MIND. I'VE GOT THIS. YOU GO CHECK ON THE OTHERS!
BUT...
GO!

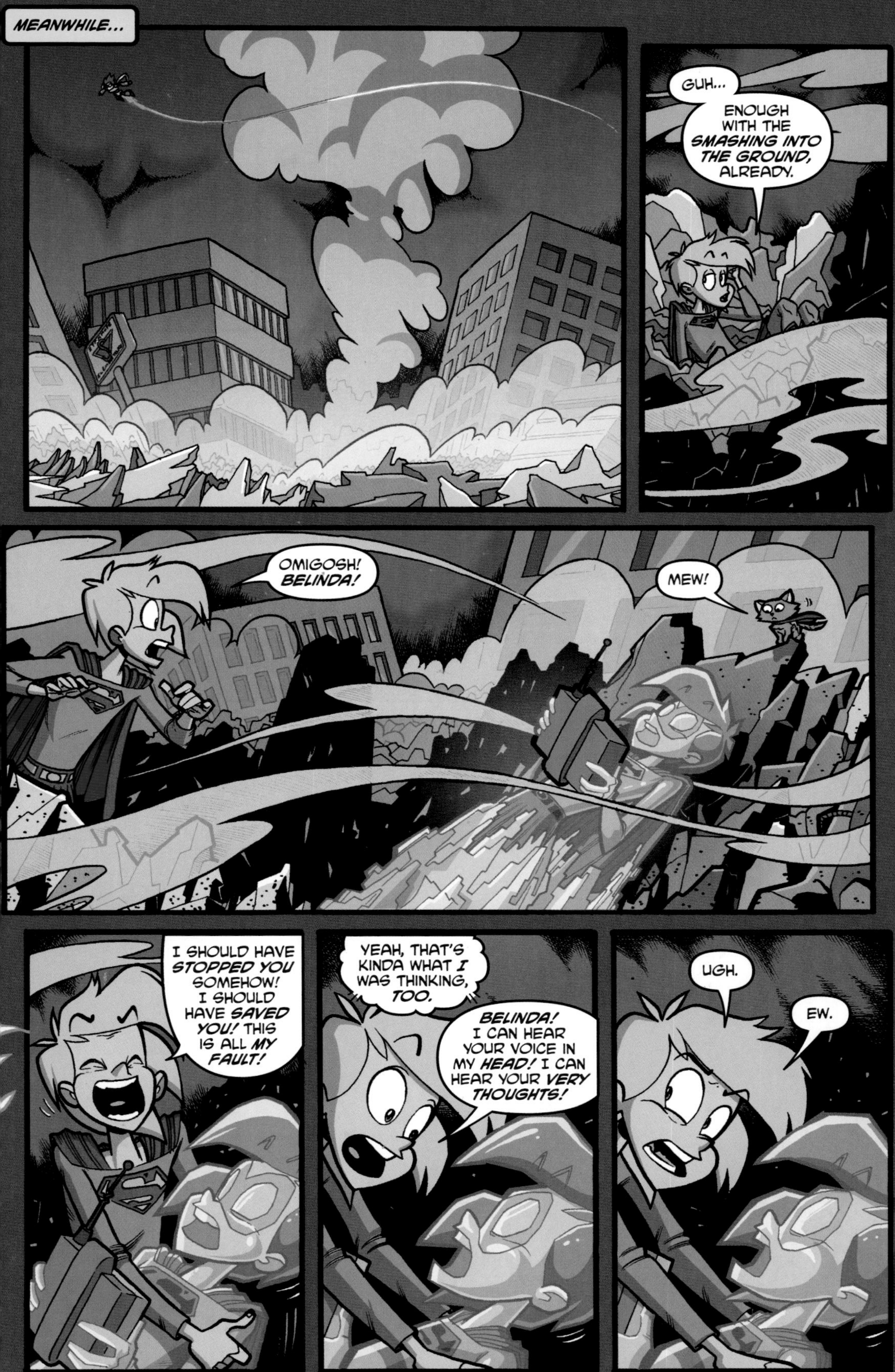

MEANWHILE...
GUH...
ENOUGH WITH THE SMASHING INTO THE GROUND, ALREADY.
OMIGOSH! BELINDA!
MEW!
I SHOULD HAVE STOPPED YOU SOMEHOW! I SHOULD HAVE SAVED YOU! THIS IS ALL MY FAULT!
YEAH, THAT'S KINDA WHAT I WAS THINKING, TOO.
BELINDA! I CAN HEAR YOUR VOICE IN MY HEAD! I CAN HEAR YOUR VERY THOUGHTS!
UGH.
EW.

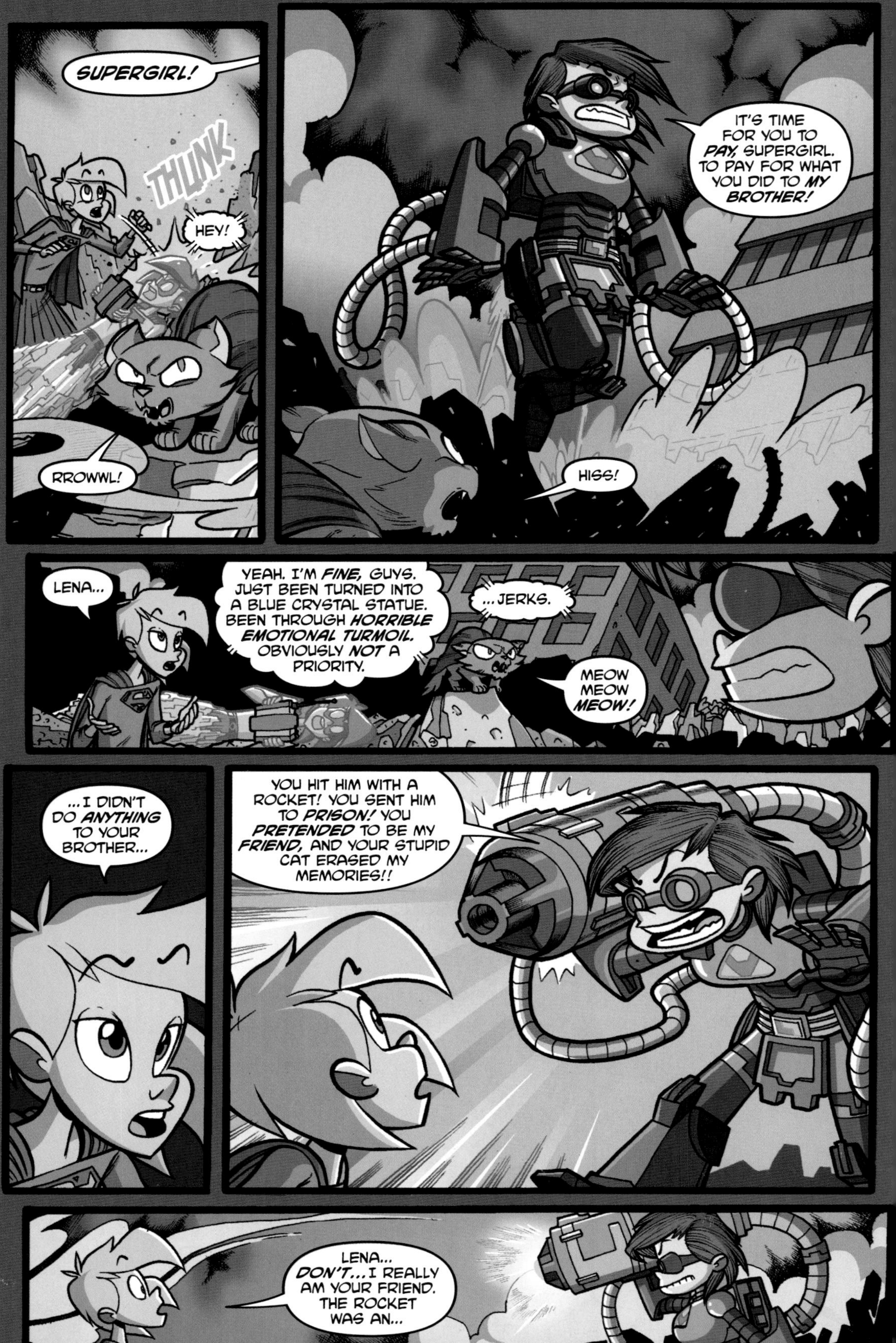
SUPERGIRL!
THUNK
HEY!
RROWWL!
IT'S TIME FOR YOU TO PAY, SUPERGIRL. TO PAY FOR WHAT YOU DID TO MY BROTHER!
HISS!
LENA...
YEAH. I'M FINE, GUYS. JUST BEEN TURNED INTO A BLUE CRYSTAL STATUE. BEEN THROUGH HORRIBLE EMOTIONAL TURMOIL. OBVIOUSLY NOT A PRIORITY.
...JERKS.
MEOW MEOW MEOW!
...I DIDN'T DO ANYTHING TO YOUR BROTHER...
YOU HIT HIM WITH A ROCKET! YOU SENT HIM TO PRISON! YOU PRETENDED TO BE MY FRIEND, AND YOUR STUPID CAT ERASED MY MEMORIES!!
LENA... DON'T... I REALLY AM YOUR FRIEND. THE ROCKET WAS AN...

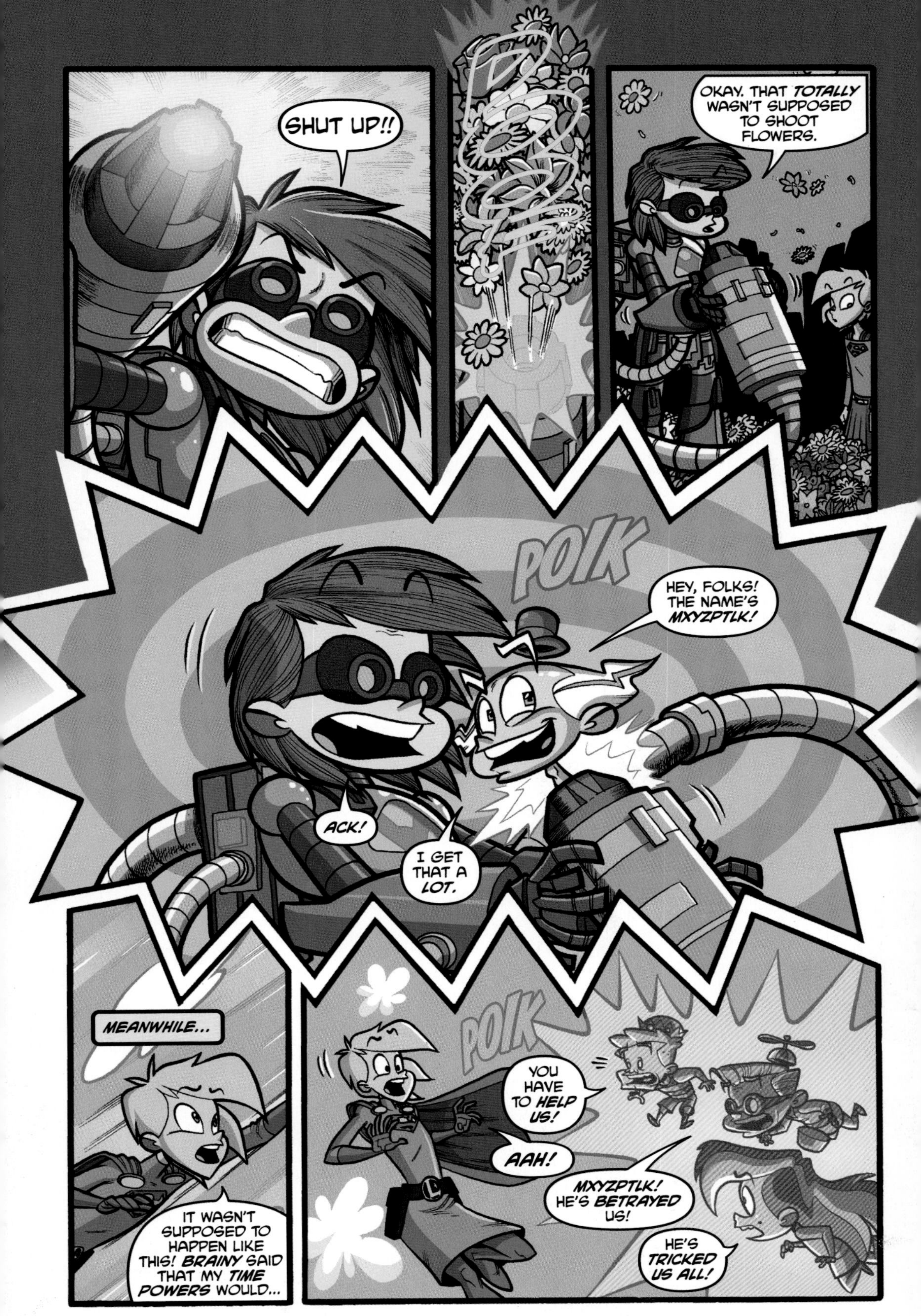
SHUT UP!!
OKAY. THAT TOTALLY WASN'T SUPPOSED TO SHOOT FLOWERS.
POIK
HEY, FOLKS! THE NAME'S MXYZPTLK!
ACK!
I GET THAT A LOT.
MEANWHILE...
IT WASN'T SUPPOSED TO HAPPEN LIKE THIS! BRAINY SAID THAT MY TIME POWERS WOULD...
POIK
YOU HAVE TO HELP US!
AAH!
MXYZPTLK! HE'S BETRAYED US!
HE'S TRICKED US ALL!

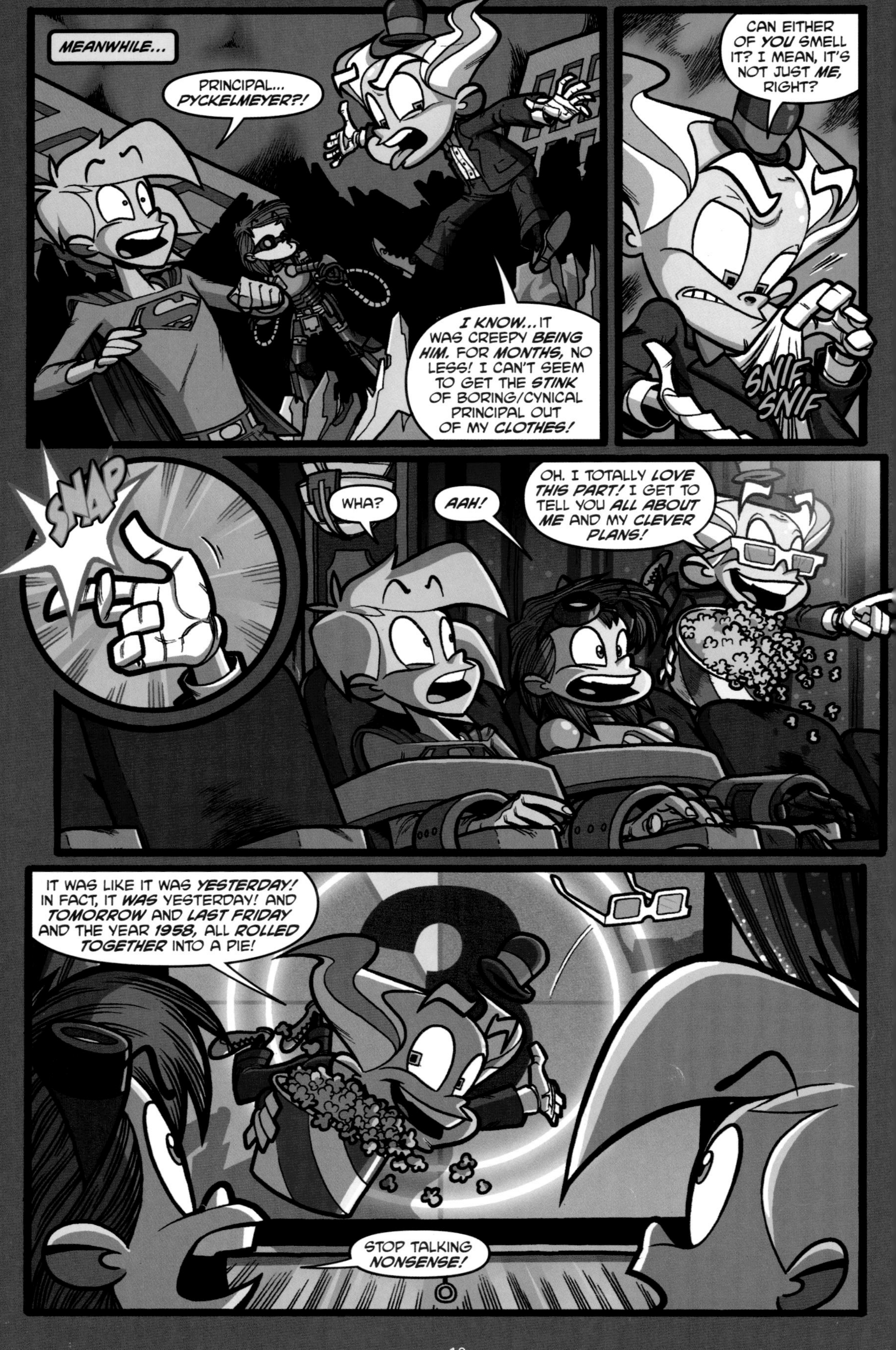
MEANWHILE...
PRINCIPAL... PYCKELMEYER?!
I KNOW... IT WAS CREEPY BEING HIM. FOR MONTHS, NO LESS! I CAN'T SEEM TO GET THE STINK OF BORING/CYNICAL PRINCIPAL OUT OF MY CLOTHES!
CAN EITHER OF YOU SMELL IT? I MEAN, IT'S NOT JUST ME, RIGHT?
SNIF SNIF
SNAP
WHA?
AAH!
OH. I TOTALLY LOVE THIS PART! I GET TO TELL YOU ALL ABOUT ME AND MY CLEVER PLANS!
IT WAS LIKE IT WAS YESTERDAY! IN FACT, IT WAS YESTERDAY! AND TOMORROW AND LAST FRIDAY AND THE YEAR 1958, ALL ROLLED TOGETHER INTO A PIE!
STOP TALKING NONSENSE!

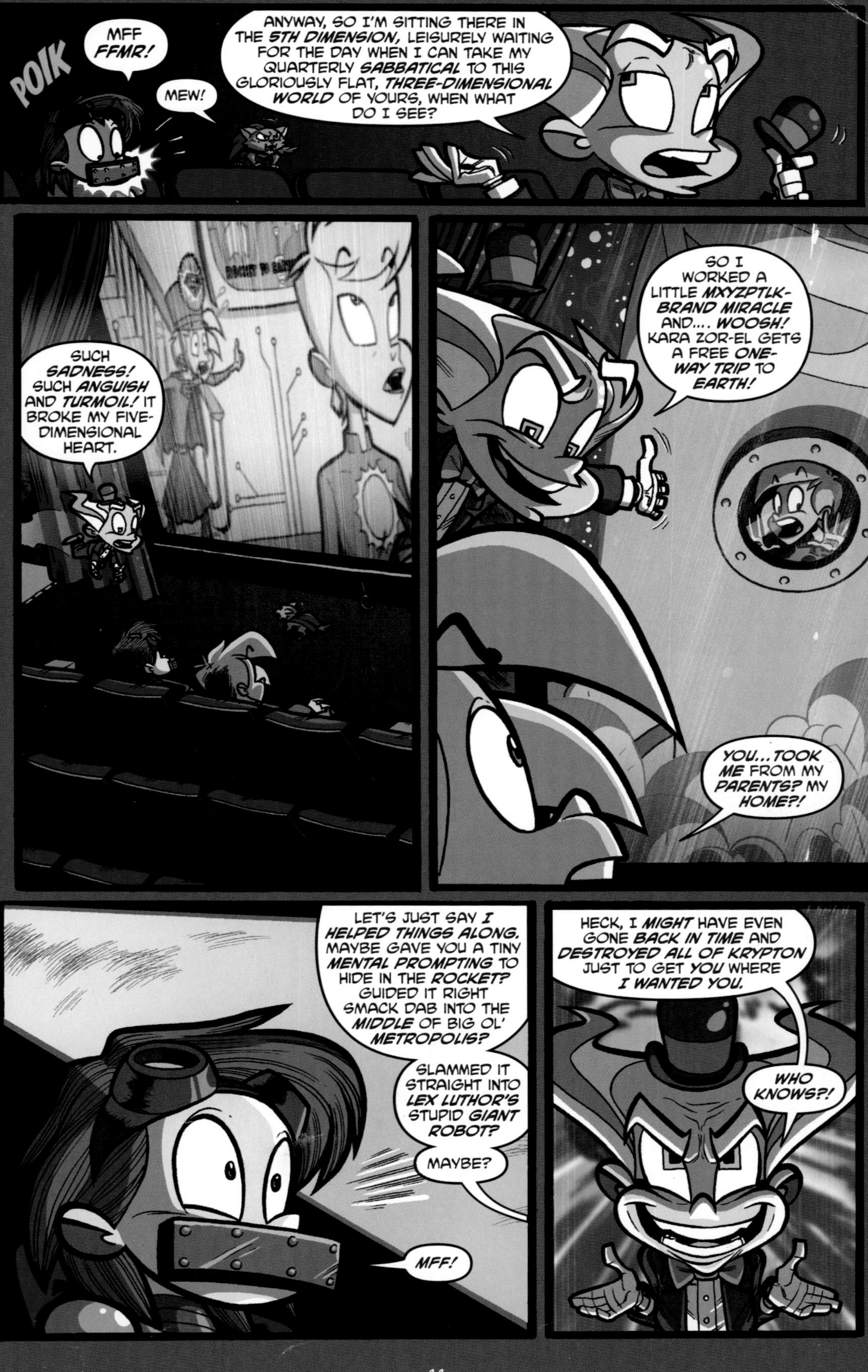
POIK
MFF FFMR!
MEW!
ANYWAY, SO I'M SITTING THERE IN THE 5TH DIMENSION, LEISURELY WAITING FOR THE DAY WHEN I CAN TAKE MY QUARTERLY SABBATICAL TO THIS GLORIOUSLY FLAT, THREE-DIMENSIONAL WORLD OF YOURS, WHEN WHAT DO I SEE?
SUCH SADNESS! SUCH ANGUISH AND TURMOIL! IT BROKE MY FIVE-DIMENSIONAL HEART.
SO I WORKED A LITTLE MXYZPTLK-BRAND MIRACLE AND.... WOOSH! KARA ZOR-EL GETS A FREE ONE-WAY TRIP TO EARTH!
YOU...TOOK ME FROM MY PARENTS? MY HOME?!
LET'S JUST SAY I HELPED THINGS ALONG. MAYBE GAVE YOU A TINY MENTAL PROMPTING TO HIDE IN THE ROCKET? GUIDED IT RIGHT SMACK DAB INTO THE MIDDLE OF BIG OL' METROPOLIS?
SLAMMED IT STRAIGHT INTO LEX LUTHOR'S STUPID GIANT ROBOT?
MAYBE?
MFF!
HECK, I MIGHT HAVE EVEN GONE BACK IN TIME AND DESTROYED ALL OF KRYPTON JUST TO GET YOU WHERE I WANTED YOU.
WHO KNOWS?!

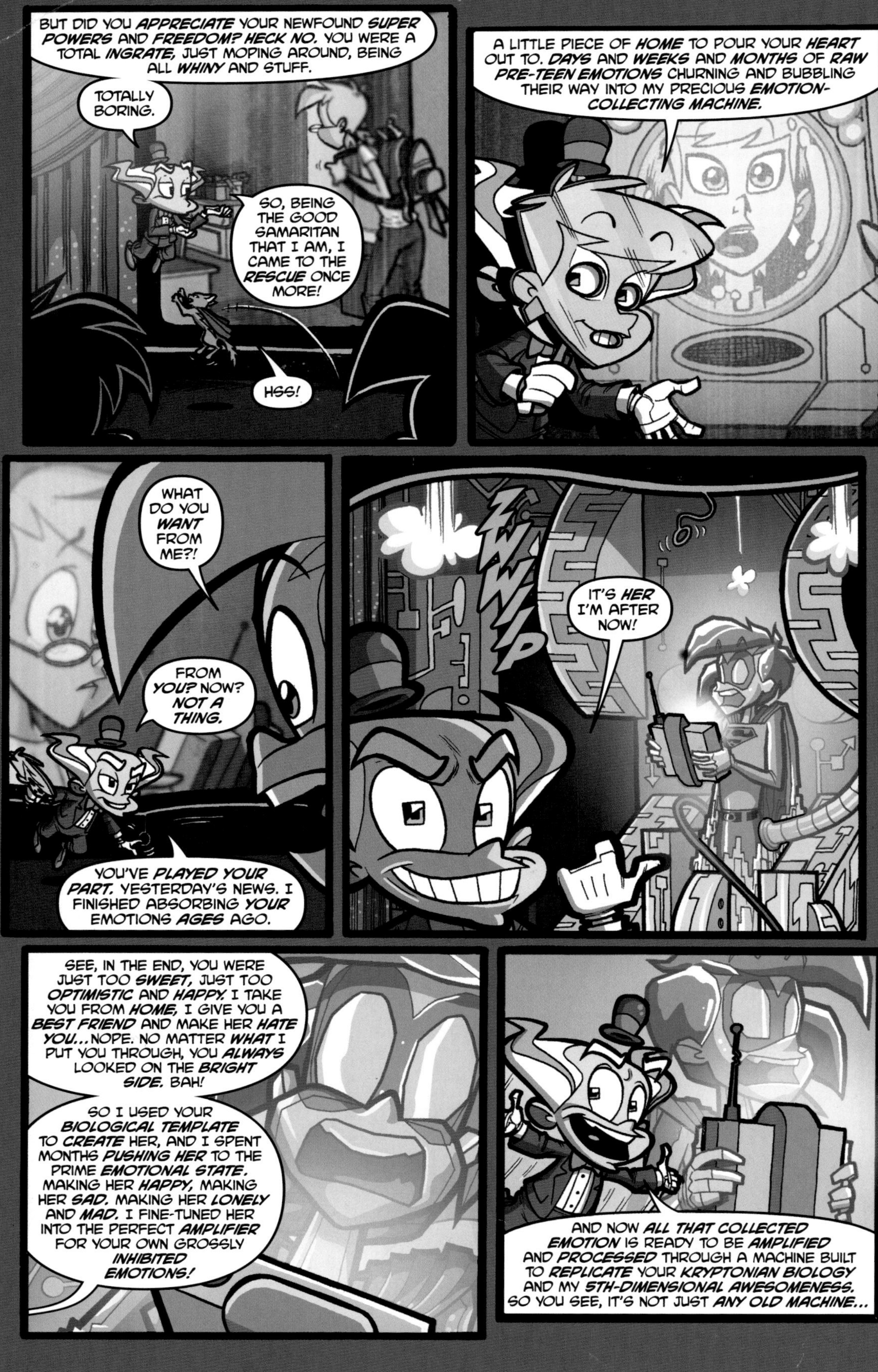

BUT DID YOU APPRECIATE YOUR NEWFOUND SUPER POWERS AND FREEDOM? HECK NO. YOU WERE A TOTAL INGRATE, JUST MOPING AROUND, BEING ALL WHINY AND STUFF.
TOTALLY BORING.
SO, BEING THE GOOD SAMARITAN THAT I AM, I CAME TO THE RESCUE ONCE MORE!
HSS!
A LITTLE PIECE OF HOME TO POUR YOUR HEART OUT TO. DAYS AND WEEKS AND MONTHS OF RAW PRE-TEEN EMOTIONS CHURNING AND BUBBLING THEIR WAY INTO MY PRECIOUS EMOTION-COLLECTING MACHINE.
WHAT DO YOU WANT FROM ME?!
FROM YOU? NOW? NOT A THING.
YOU'VE PLAYED YOUR PART. YESTERDAY'S NEWS. I FINISHED ABSORBING YOUR EMOTIONS AGES AGO.
ZWWIP
IT'S HER I'M AFTER NOW!
SEE, IN THE END, YOU WERE JUST TOO SWEET, JUST TOO OPTIMISTIC AND HAPPY. I TAKE YOU FROM HOME, I GIVE YOU A BEST FRIEND AND MAKE HER HATE YOU...NOPE. NO MATTER WHAT I PUT YOU THROUGH, YOU ALWAYS LOOKED ON THE BRIGHT SIDE. BAH!
SO I USED YOUR BIOLOGICAL TEMPLATE TO CREATE HER, AND I SPENT MONTHS PUSHING HER TO THE PRIME EMOTIONAL STATE. MAKING HER HAPPY, MAKING HER SAD. MAKING HER LONELY AND MAD. I FINE-TUNED HER INTO THE PERFECT AMPLIFIER FOR YOUR OWN GROSSLY INHIBITED EMOTIONS!
AND NOW ALL THAT COLLECTED EMOTION IS READY TO BE AMPLIFIED AND PROCESSED THROUGH A MACHINE BUILT TO REPLICATE YOUR KRYPTONIAN BIOLOGY AND MY 5TH-DIMENSIONAL AWESOMENESS. SO YOU SEE, IT'S NOT JUST ANY OLD MACHINE...

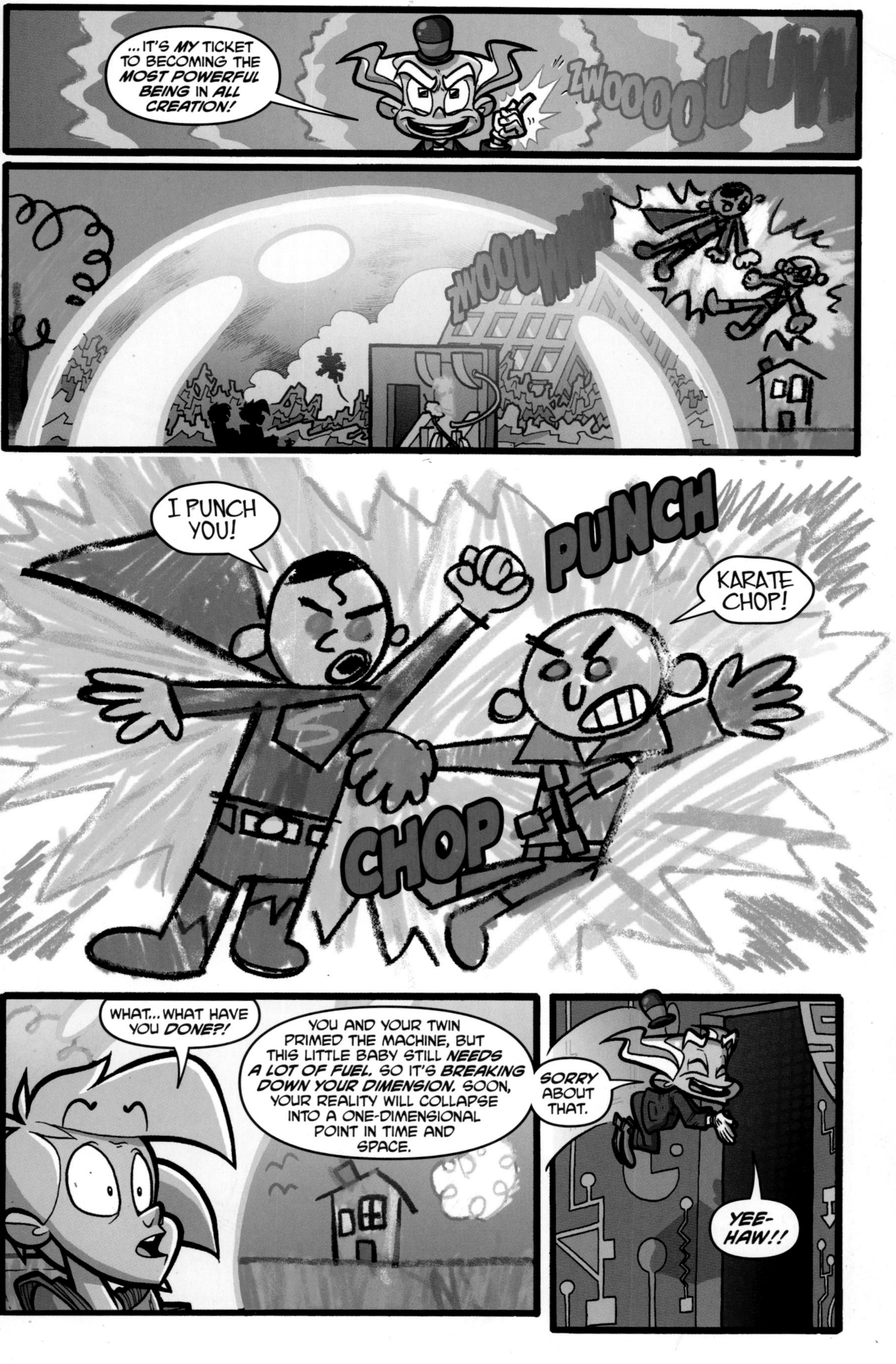
...IT'S MY TICKET TO BECOMING THE MOST POWERFUL BEING IN ALL CREATION!
ZWOOOOOUUUW
ZWOOUWWW!!
I PUNCH YOU!
PUNCH
KARATE CHOP!
CHOP
WHAT...WHAT HAVE YOU DONE?!
YOU AND YOUR TWIN PRIMED THE MACHINE, BUT THIS LITTLE BABY STILL NEEDS A LOT OF FUEL. SO IT'S BREAKING DOWN YOUR DIMENSION. SOON, YOUR REALITY WILL COLLAPSE INTO A ONE-DIMENSIONAL POINT IN TIME AND SPACE.
SORRY ABOUT THAT.
YEE-HAW!!

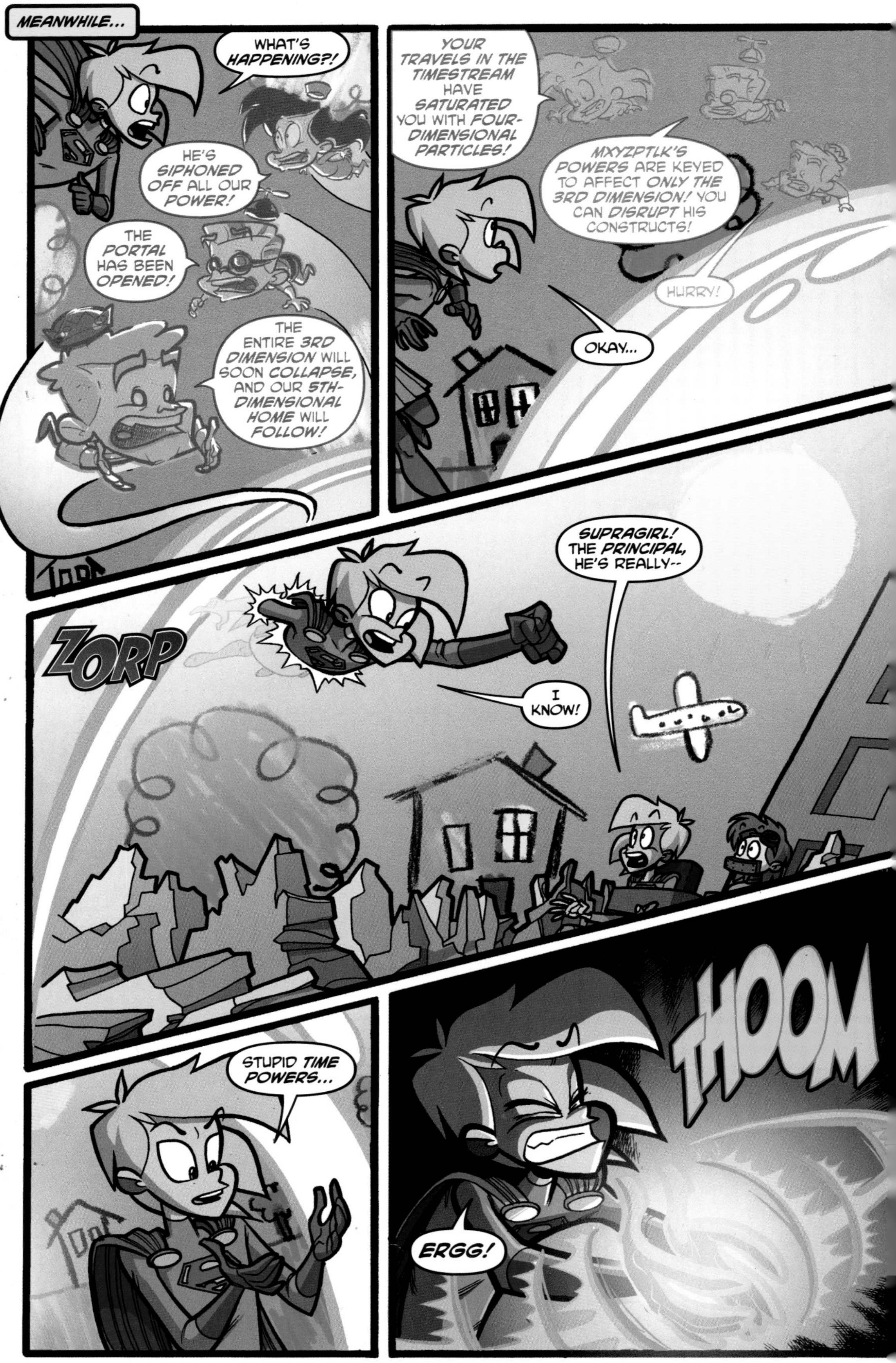
MEANWHILE...
WHAT'S HAPPENING?!
HE'S SIPHONED OFF ALL OUR POWER!
THE PORTAL HAS BEEN OPENED!
THE ENTIRE 3RD DIMENSION WILL SOON COLLAPSE, AND OUR 5TH-DIMENSIONAL HOME WILL FOLLOW!
YOUR TRAVELS IN THE TIMESTREAM HAVE SATURATED YOU WITH FOUR-DIMENSIONAL PARTICLES!
MXYZPTLK'S POWERS ARE KEYED TO AFFECT ONLY THE 3RD DIMENSION! YOU CAN DISRUPT HIS CONSTRUCTS!
HURRY!
OKAY...
SUPRAGIRL! THE PRINCIPAL, HE'S REALLY--
ZORP
I KNOW!
STUPID TIME POWERS...
THOOM
ERGG!

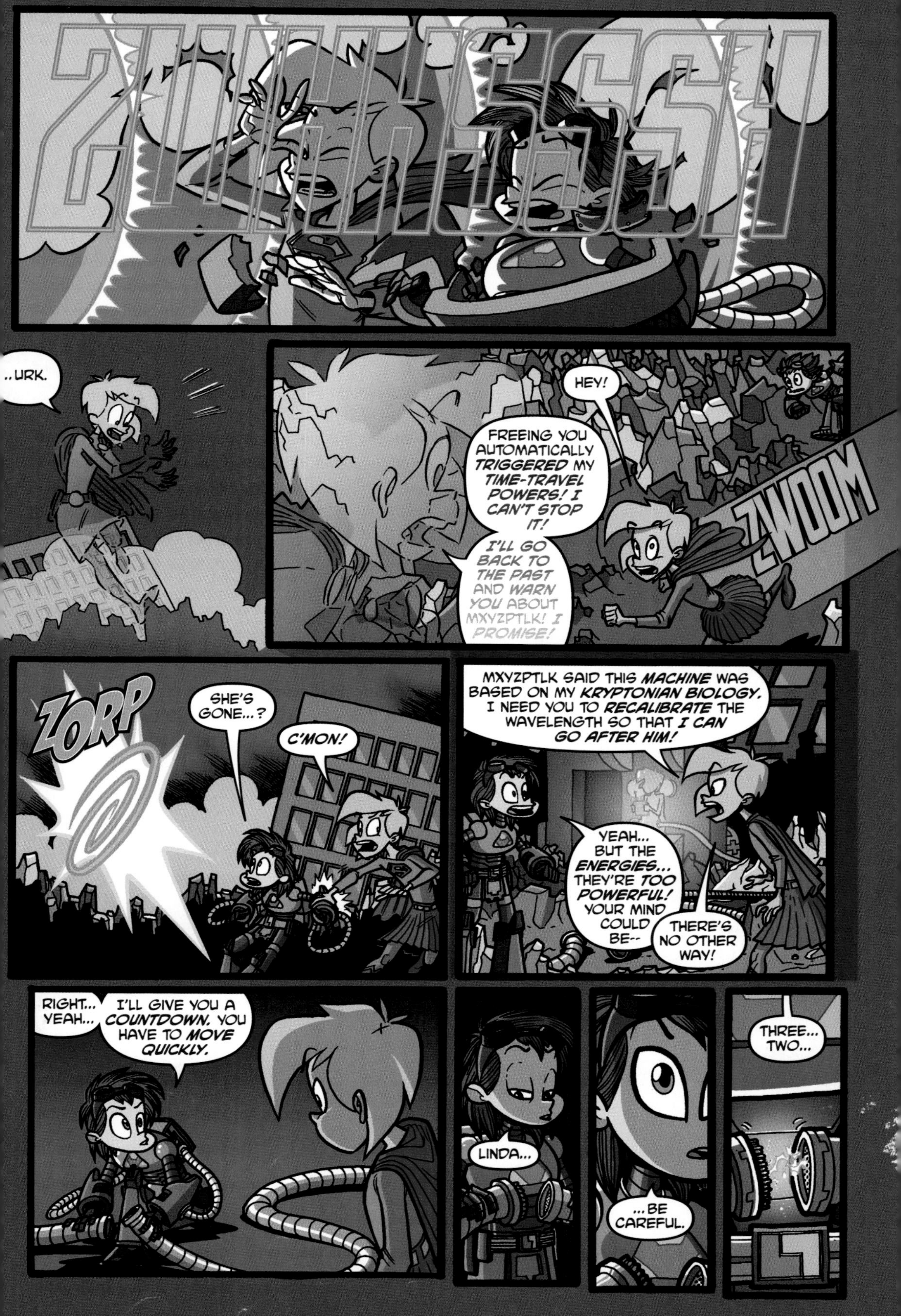
ZZHHHSSSH!
..URK.
HEY!
FREEING YOU AUTOMATICALLY TRIGGERED MY TIME-TRAVEL POWERS! I CAN'T STOP IT!
I'LL GO BACK TO THE PAST AND WARN YOU ABOUT MXYZPTLK! I PROMISE!
ZWOOM
ZORP
SHE'S GONE...?
C'MON!
MXYZPTLK SAID THIS MACHINE WAS BASED ON MY KRYPTONIAN BIOLOGY. I NEED YOU TO RECALIBRATE THE WAVELENGTH SO THAT I CAN GO AFTER HIM!
YEAH... BUT THE ENERGIES... THEY'RE TOO POWERFUL! YOUR MIND COULD BE--
THERE'S NO OTHER WAY!
RIGHT... YEAH...
I'LL GIVE YOU A COUNTDOWN. YOU HAVE TO MOVE QUICKLY.
LINDA...
...BE CAREFUL.
THREE... TWO...

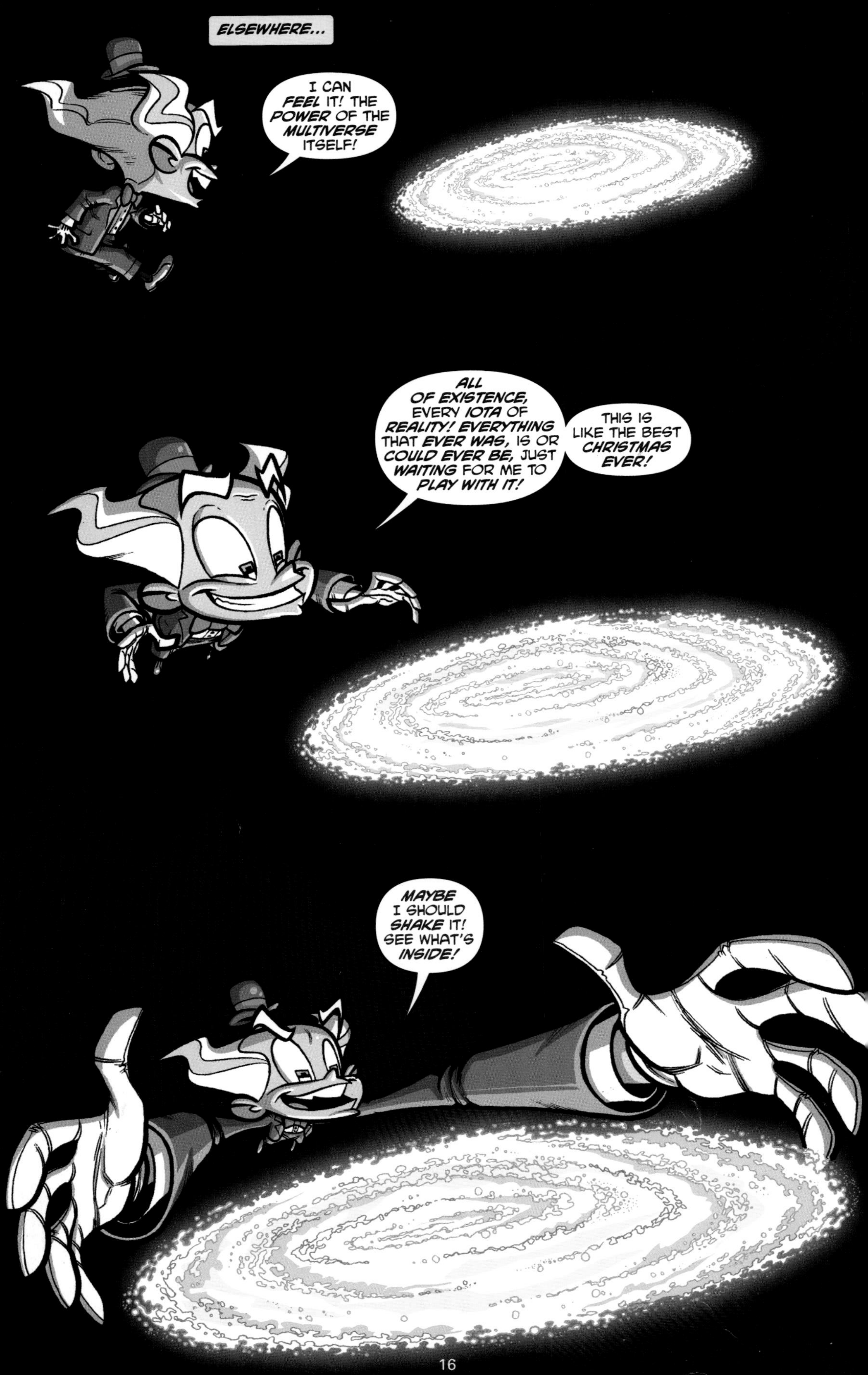
ELSEWHERE...
I CAN FEEL IT! THE POWER OF THE MULTIVERSE ITSELF!
ALL OF EXISTENCE, EVERY IOTA OF REALITY! EVERYTHING THAT EVER WAS, IS OR COULD EVER BE, JUST WAITING FOR ME TO PLAY WITH IT!
THIS IS LIKE THE BEST CHRISTMAS EVER!
MAYBE I SHOULD SHAKE IT! SEE WHAT'S INSIDE!

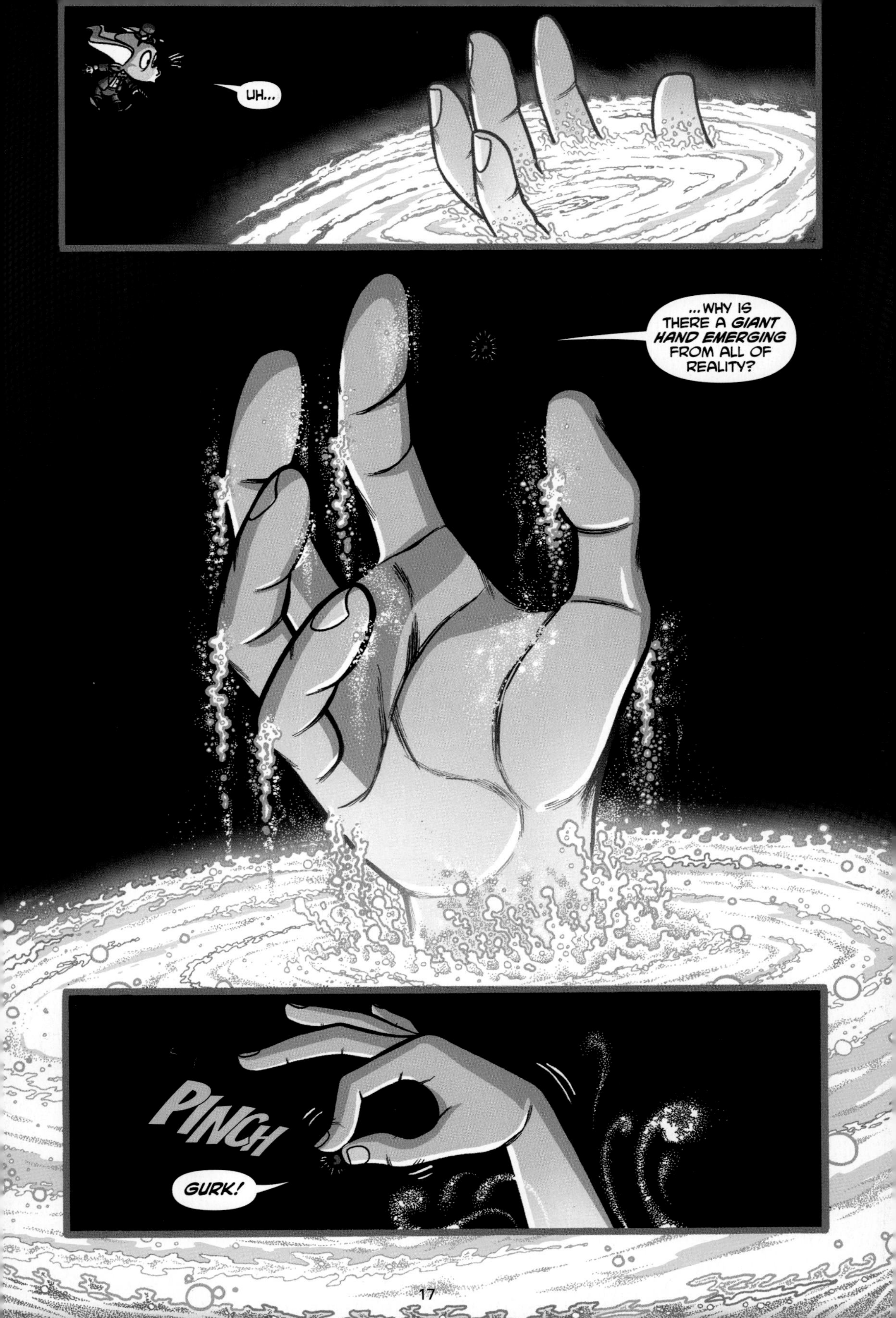
UH...
...WHY IS THERE A GIANT HAND EMERGING FROM ALL OF REALITY?
PINCH
GURK!

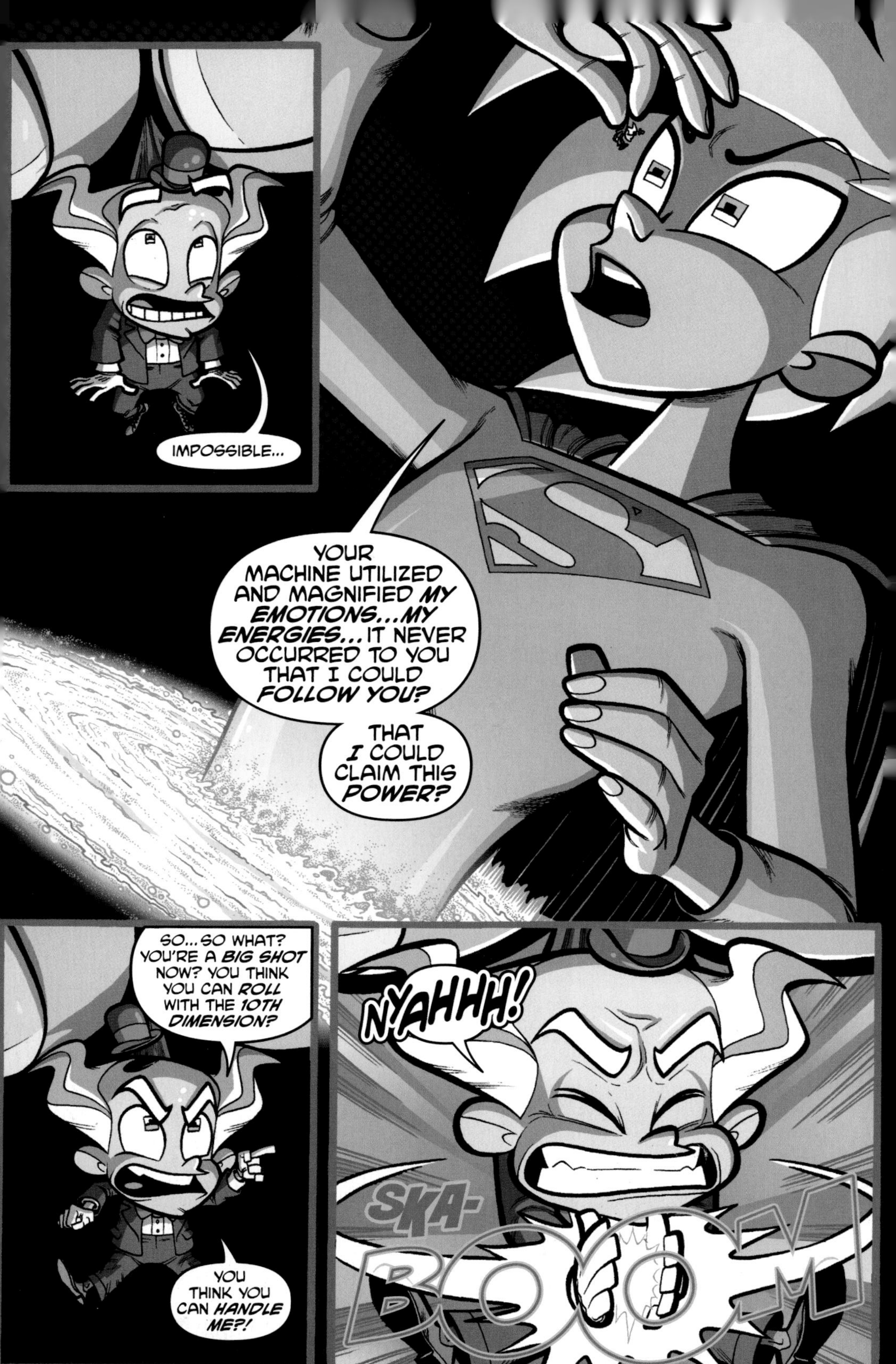
IMPOSSIBLE...
YOUR MACHINE UTILIZED AND MAGNIFIED *MY EMOTIONS...MY ENERGIES...* IT NEVER OCCURRED TO YOU THAT I COULD *FOLLOW YOU?*
THAT *I* COULD CLAIM THIS *POWER?*
SO...SO WHAT? YOU'RE A *BIG SHOT* NOW? YOU THINK YOU CAN *ROLL* WITH THE *10TH DIMENSION?*
YOU THINK YOU CAN *HANDLE ME?!*
NYAHHH!
SKA-BOOM

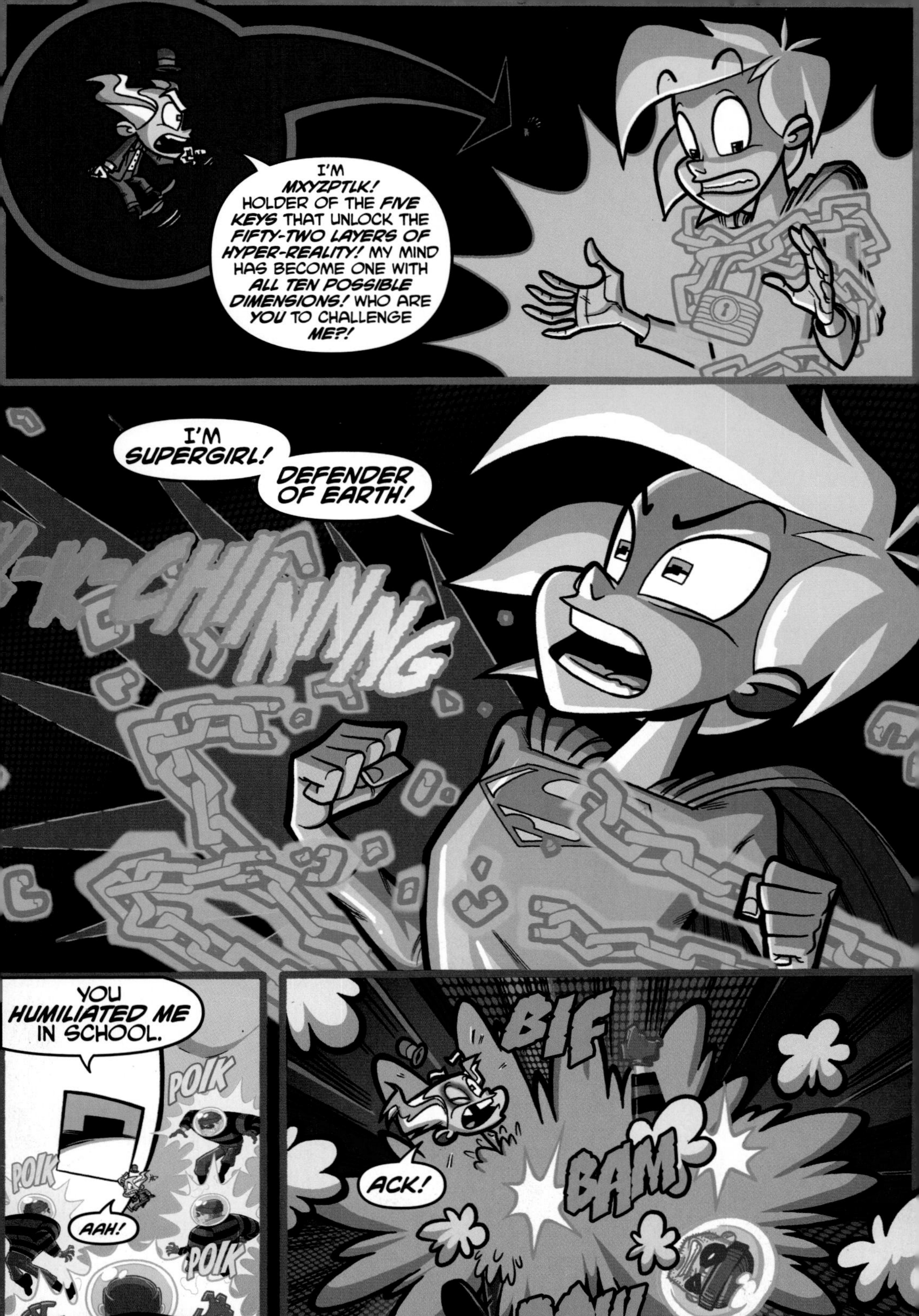

I'M MXYZPTLK! HOLDER OF THE FIVE KEYS THAT UNLOCK THE FIFTY-TWO LAYERS OF HYPER-REALITY! MY MIND HAS BECOME ONE WITH ALL TEN POSSIBLE DIMENSIONS! WHO ARE YOU TO CHALLENGE ME?!
I'M SUPERGIRL!
DEFENDER OF EARTH!
CHINNNG
YOU HUMILIATED ME IN SCHOOL.
POIK
POIK
AAH!
POIK
POIK
BIF
ACK!
BAM
POW

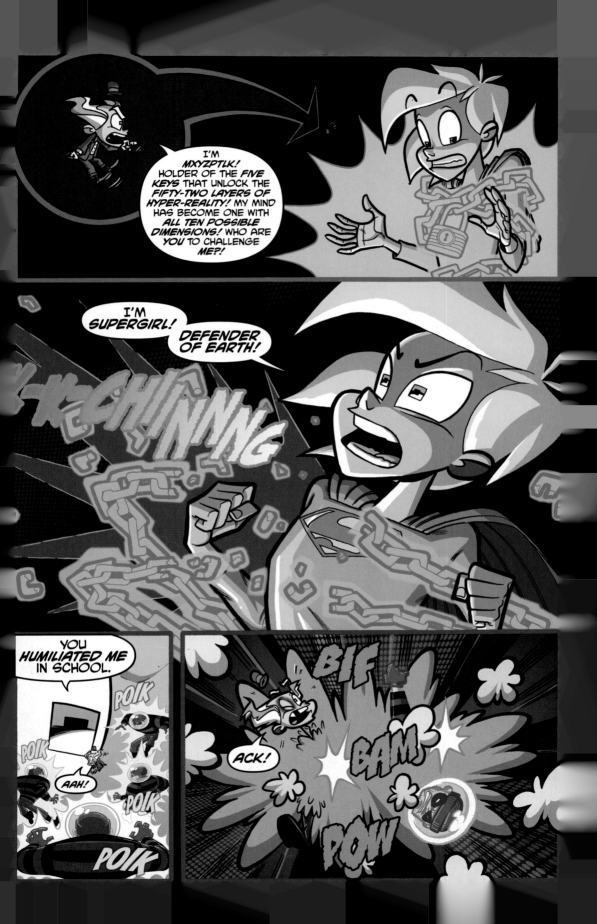

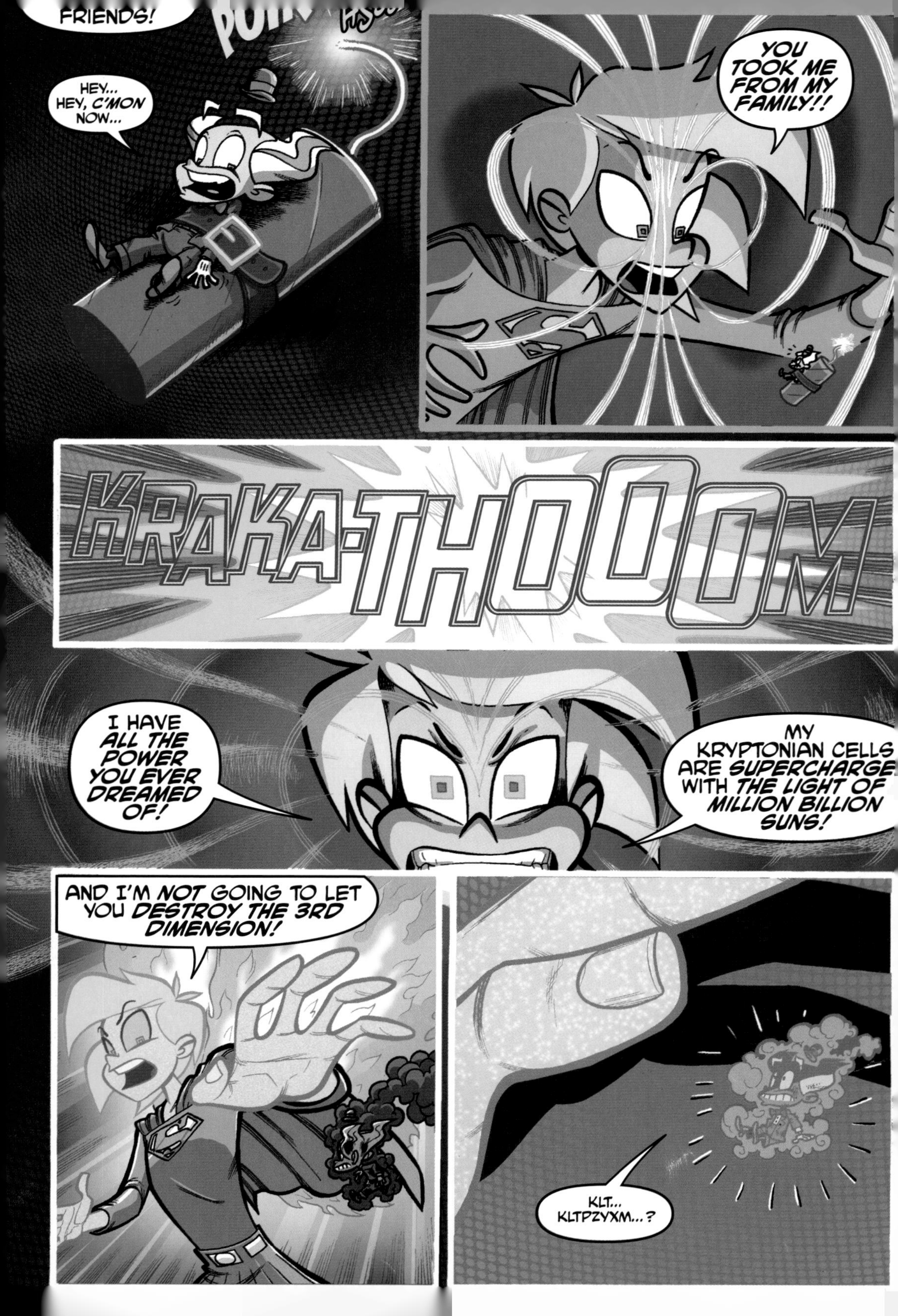
FRIENDS!
HEY... HEY, C'MON NOW...
YOU TOOK ME FROM MY FAMILY!!
KRAKA-THOOOOM
I HAVE ALL THE POWER YOU EVER DREAMED OF!
MY KRYPTONIAN CELLS ARE SUPERCHARGE WITH THE LIGHT OF MILLION BILLION SUNS!
AND I'M NOT GOING TO LET YOU DESTROY THE 3RD DIMENSION!
KLT... KLTPZYXM...?

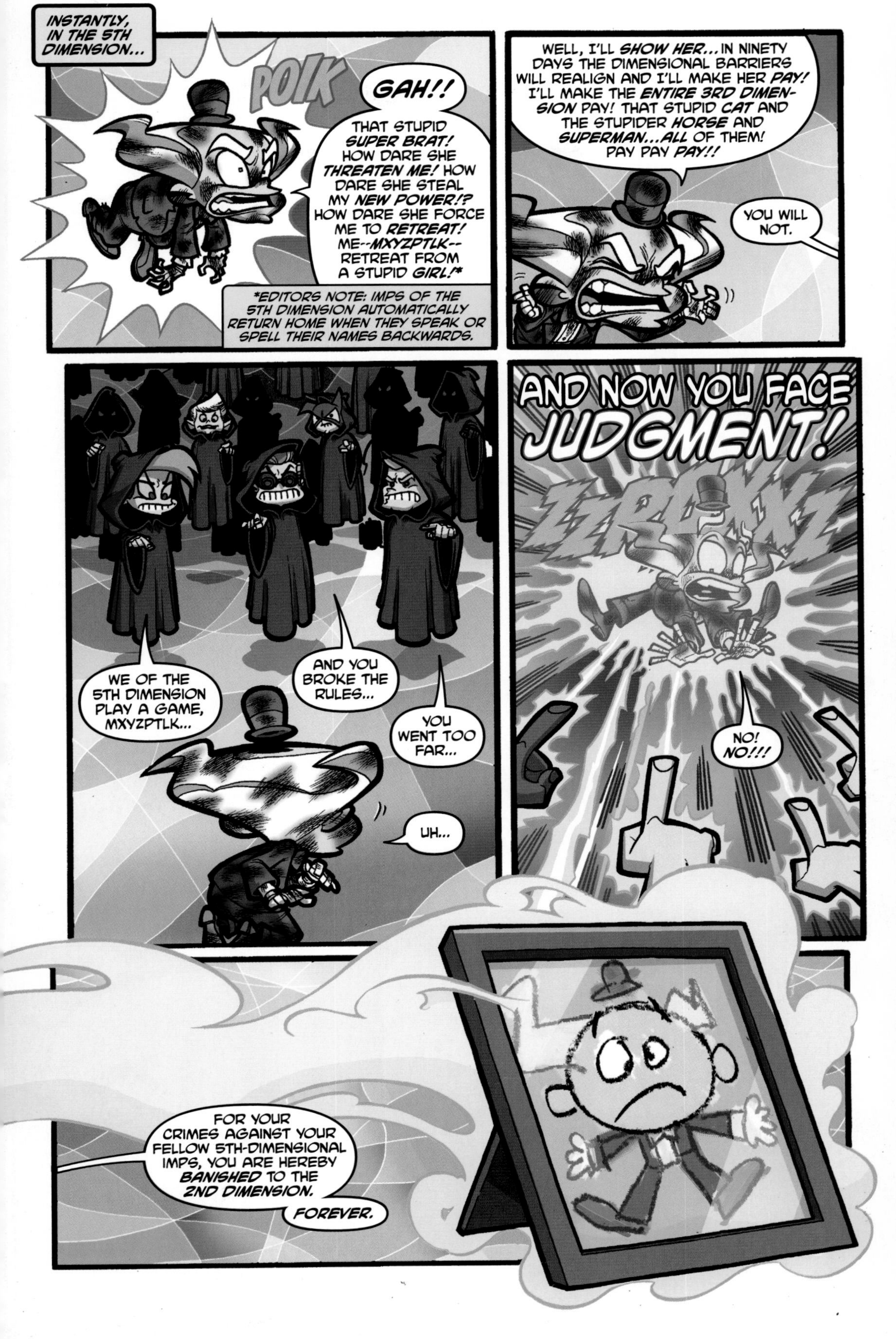
INSTANTLY, IN THE 5TH DIMENSION...
POIK
GAH!!
THAT STUPID SUPER BRAT! HOW DARE SHE THREATEN ME! HOW DARE SHE STEAL MY NEW POWER!? HOW DARE SHE FORCE ME TO RETREAT! ME--MXYZPTLK--RETREAT FROM A STUPID GIRL!*
*EDITORS NOTE: IMPS OF THE 5TH DIMENSION AUTOMATICALLY RETURN HOME WHEN THEY SPEAK OR SPELL THEIR NAMES BACKWARDS.
WELL, I'LL SHOW HER... IN NINETY DAYS THE DIMENSIONAL BARRIERS WILL REALIGN AND I'LL MAKE HER PAY! I'LL MAKE THE ENTIRE 3RD DIMENSION PAY! THAT STUPID CAT AND THE STUPIDER HORSE AND SUPERMAN...ALL OF THEM! PAY PAY PAY!!
YOU WILL NOT.
WE OF THE 5TH DIMENSION PLAY A GAME, MXYZPTLK...
AND YOU BROKE THE RULES...
YOU WENT TOO FAR...
UH...
AND NOW YOU FACE JUDGMENT!
ZZRAKZ
NO! NO!!!
FOR YOUR CRIMES AGAINST YOUR FELLOW 5TH-DIMENSIONAL IMPS, YOU ARE HEREBY BANISHED TO THE 2ND DIMENSION.
FOREVER.

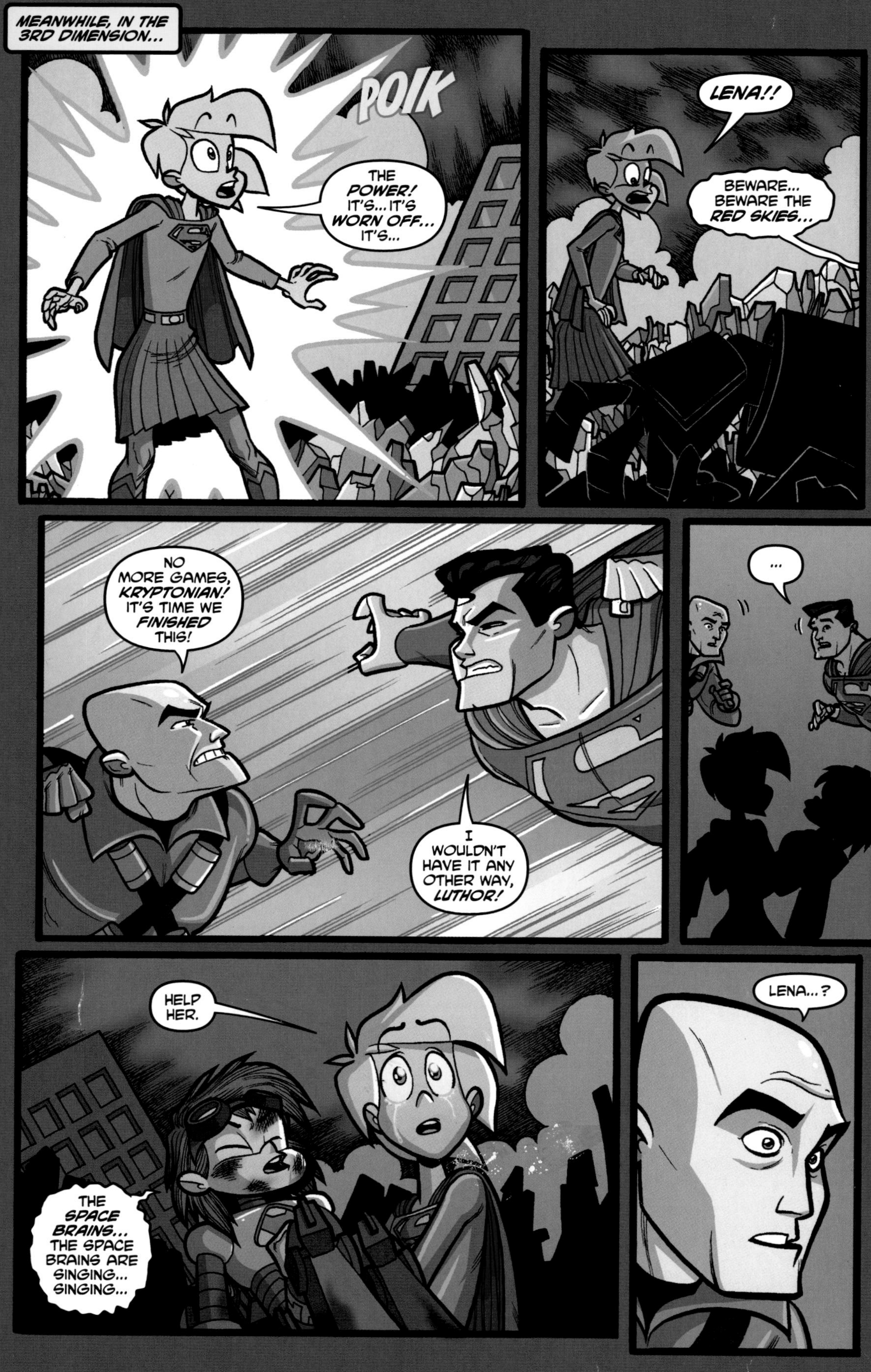
MEANWHILE, IN THE 3RD DIMENSION...
POIK
THE POWER! IT'S... IT'S WORN OFF... IT'S...
LENA!!
BEWARE... BEWARE THE RED SKIES...
NO MORE GAMES, KRYPTONIAN! IT'S TIME WE FINISHED THIS!
I WOULDN'T HAVE IT ANY OTHER WAY, LUTHOR!
...
HELP HER.
THE SPACE BRAINS... THE SPACE BRAINS ARE SINGING... SINGING...
LENA...?

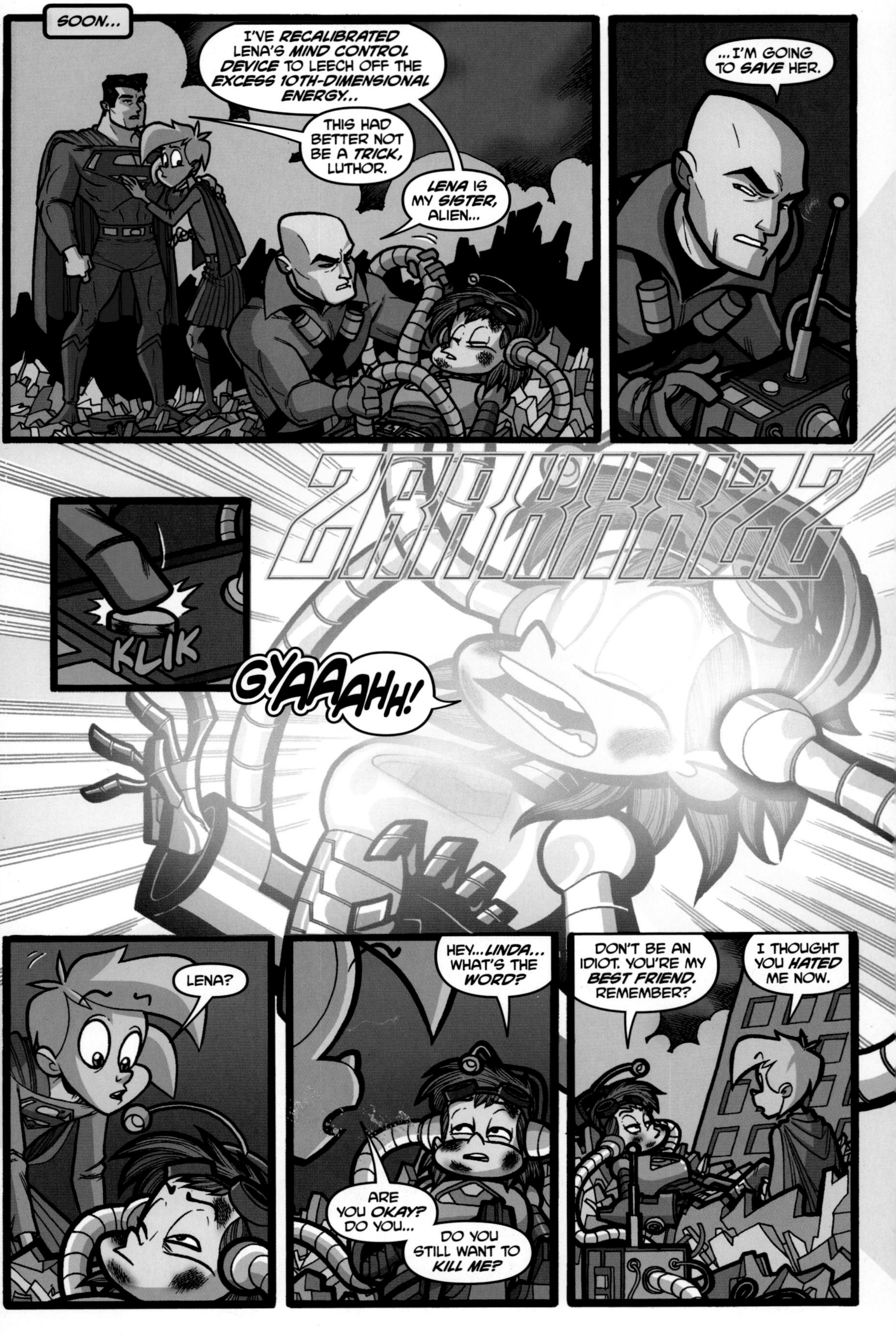

SOON...
I'VE RECALIBRATED LENA'S MIND CONTROL DEVICE TO LEECH OFF THE EXCESS 10TH-DIMENSIONAL ENERGY...
THIS HAD BETTER NOT BE A TRICK, LUTHOR.
LENA IS MY SISTER, ALIEN...
...I'M GOING TO SAVE HER.
KLIK
ZRRKKKZZ
GYAAAHH!
LENA?
HEY...LINDA... WHAT'S THE WORD?
ARE YOU OKAY? DO YOU...
DO YOU STILL WANT TO KILL ME?
DON'T BE AN IDIOT. YOU'RE MY BEST FRIEND. REMEMBER?
I THOUGHT YOU HATED ME NOW.

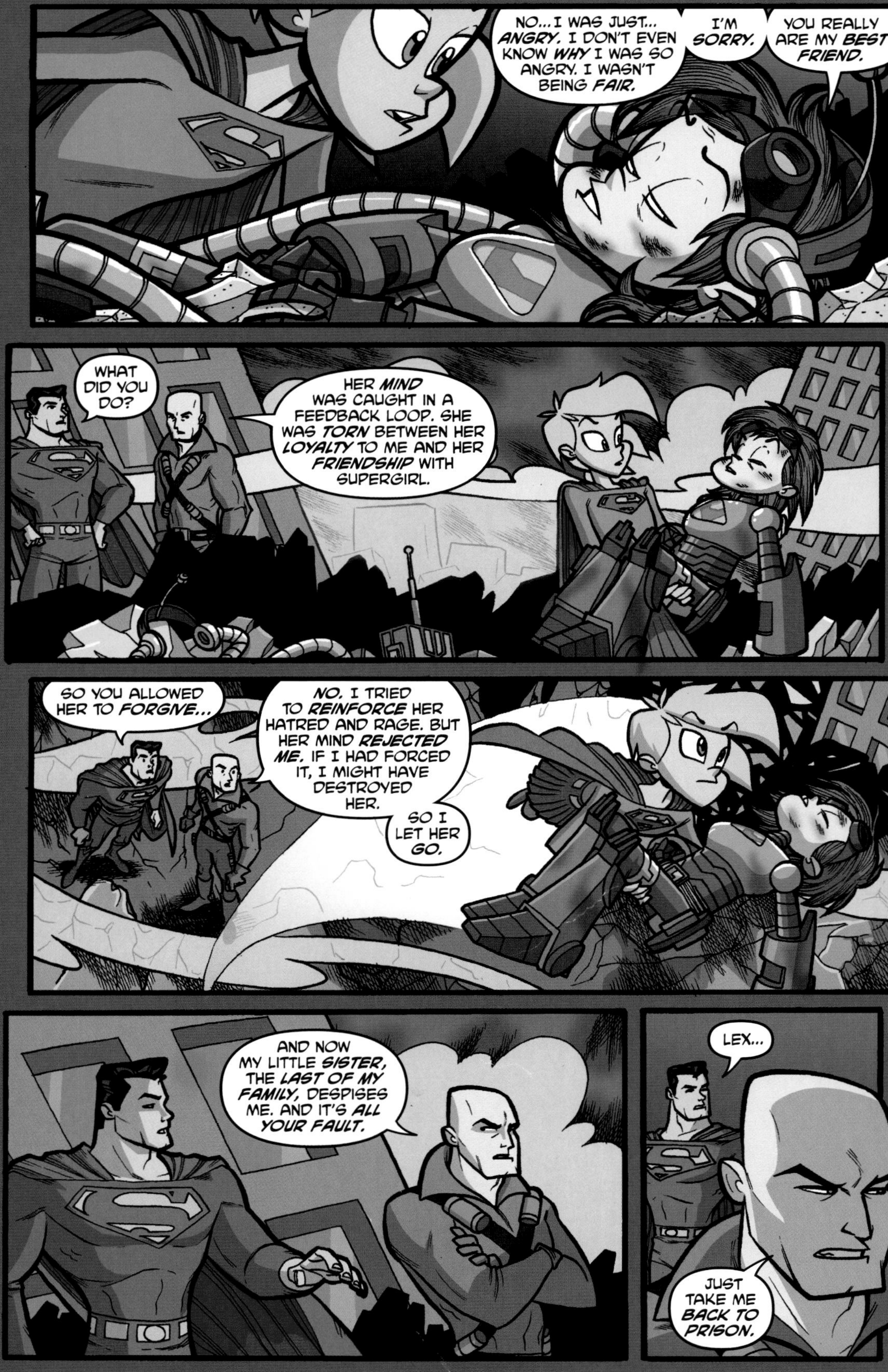
NO... I WAS JUST... ANGRY. I DON'T EVEN KNOW WHY I WAS SO ANGRY. I WASN'T BEING FAIR.
I'M SORRY.
YOU REALLY ARE MY BEST FRIEND.
WHAT DID YOU DO?
HER MIND WAS CAUGHT IN A FEEDBACK LOOP. SHE WAS TORN BETWEEN HER LOYALTY TO ME AND HER FRIENDSHIP WITH SUPERGIRL.
SO YOU ALLOWED HER TO FORGIVE...
NO. I TRIED TO REINFORCE HER HATRED AND RAGE. BUT HER MIND REJECTED ME. IF I HAD FORCED IT, I MIGHT HAVE DESTROYED HER.
SO I LET HER GO.
AND NOW MY LITTLE SISTER, THE LAST OF MY FAMILY, DESPISES ME. AND IT'S ALL YOUR FAULT.
LEX...
JUST TAKE ME BACK TO PRISON.

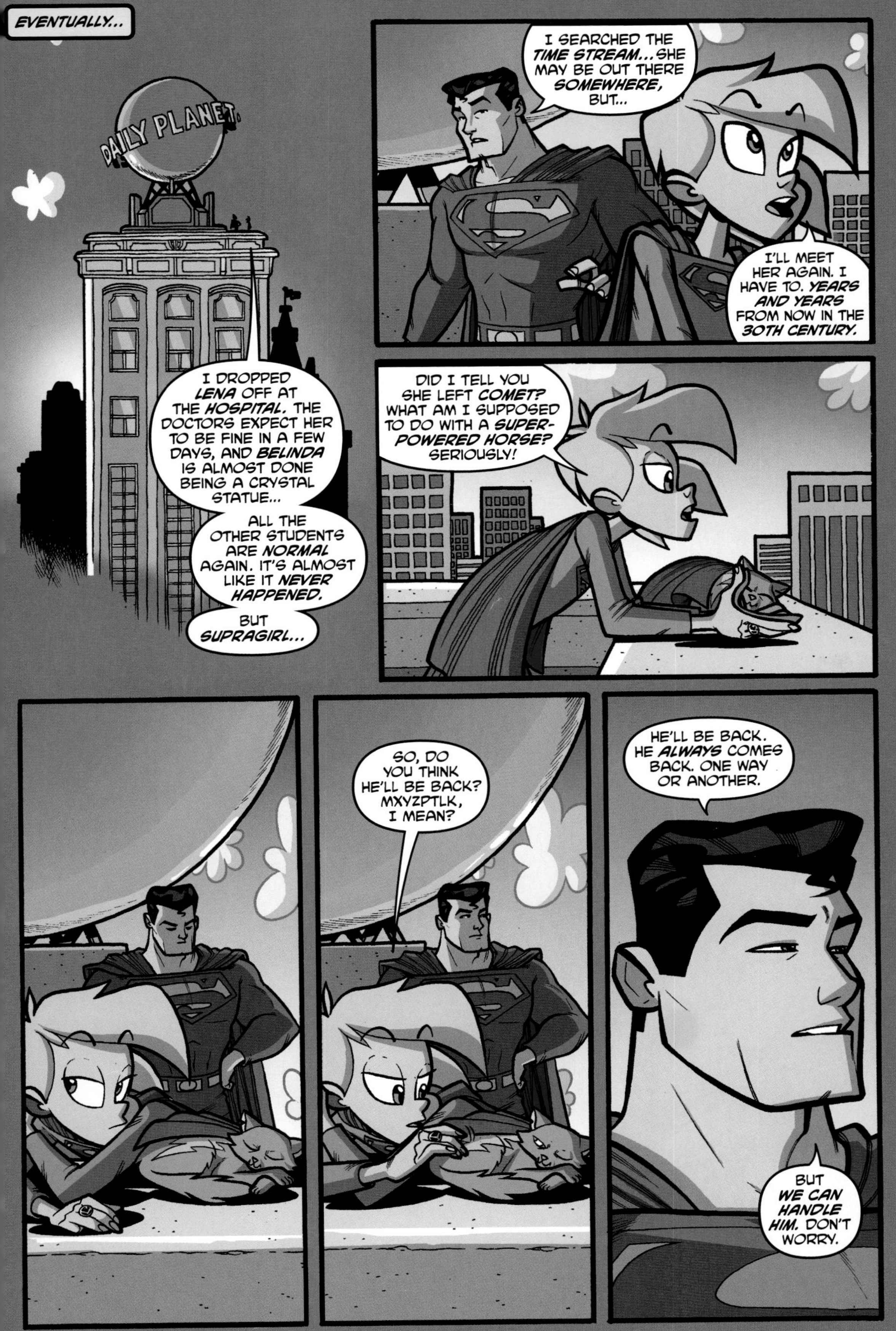
EVENTUALLY...
DAILY PLANET
I DROPPED LENA OFF AT THE HOSPITAL. THE DOCTORS EXPECT HER TO BE FINE IN A FEW DAYS, AND BELINDA IS ALMOST DONE BEING A CRYSTAL STATUE...
ALL THE OTHER STUDENTS ARE NORMAL AGAIN. IT'S ALMOST LIKE IT NEVER HAPPENED.
BUT SUPRAGIRL...
I SEARCHED THE TIME STREAM...SHE MAY BE OUT THERE SOMEWHERE, BUT...
I'LL MEET HER AGAIN. I HAVE TO. YEARS AND YEARS FROM NOW IN THE 30TH CENTURY.
DID I TELL YOU SHE LEFT COMET? WHAT AM I SUPPOSED TO DO WITH A SUPER-POWERED HORSE? SERIOUSLY!
SO, DO YOU THINK HE'LL BE BACK? MXYZPTLK, I MEAN?
HE'LL BE BACK. HE ALWAYS COMES BACK. ONE WAY OR ANOTHER.
BUT WE CAN HANDLE HIM. DON'T WORRY.

OH! I ALMOST FORGOT... I HAVE SOMETHING FOR YOU.

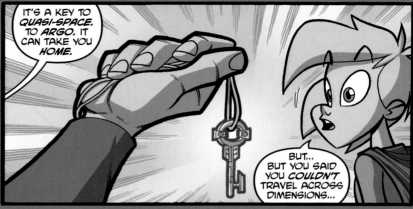

IT'S A KEY TO *QUASI-SPACE*. TO *ARGO*. IT CAN TAKE YOU *HOME*.

BUT... BUT YOU SAID YOU *COULDN'T* TRAVEL ACROSS DIMENSIONS...

I CAN'T. BUT *YOU* CAN. IT JUST TOOK ME A WHILE TO FIGURE OUT HOW TO *HELP YOU ALONG*.

OF COURSE, *YOU* COULD HAVE TAKEN YOURSELF HOME WHEN YOU WERE FIGHTING MXYZPTLK. YOU HAD THE POWER *THEN*.

I WAS KINDA *DISTRACTED*...

THIS WILL *REALLY* TAKE ME *HOME*?

ANYTIME YOU WANT.

WELL... MAYBE *LATER*, THEN...

RIGHT NOW *WE HAVE* A PLANET TO *PROTECT*.

DAILY PLANET

The End!

26

CREATORS

LANDRY Q. WALKER WRITER

Landry Q. Walker is a comics writer whose projects include *Supergirl: Cosmic Adventures in the 8th Grade* and more. He has also written *Batman: The Brave and the Bold*, the comic book adventures of The Incredibles, and contributed stories to *Disney Adventures* magazine and the gaming website Elder-Geek.

ERIC JONES ARTIST

Eric Jones is a professional comic book artist whose work for DC Comics include *Batman: The Brave and the Bold*, *Supergirl: Cosmic Adventures in the 8th Grade*, *Cartoon Network Action Pack*, and more.

JOEY MASON COLORIST

Joey Mason is an illustrator, animation artist, and comic book colorist. His work for DC Comics includes *Supergirl: Cosmic Adventures in the 8th Grade*, as well as set designs for *Green Lantern: The Animated Series*.

GLOSSARY

anguish [ANG-gwish]—a strong feeling of misery or distress
clever [KLEV-ur]—able to understand things and do things quickly and easily, or intelligently and carefully thought out
cynical [SIN-uh-kuhl]—someone who is cynical always expects the worst to happen and thinks that anything people do is for selfish reasons
distracted [diss-TRAKT-id]—weakened someone's concentration
humiliated [hyoo-MIL-ee-ate-id]—made someone look or feel foolish or embarrassed
ingrate [IN-grait]—an ungrateful person
inhibited [in-HIB-it-tid]—held in check, or prevented from doing something
optimistic [op-tuh-MISS-tik]—people who are optimistic always believe that things will turn out for the best
priority [prye-OR-uh-tee]—something that is more important or more urgent than other things
reinforce [ree-in-FORSS]—strengthen or add support to
saturated [SACH-uh-rate-id]—soaked thoroughly or filled completely
turmoil [TUR-moil]—great confusion and agitation

VISUAL QUESTIONS & PROMPTS

1. Based on what you know from the story, who made Lena's gun shoot flowers, and why?

OKAY. THAT *TOTALLY* WASN'T SUPPOSED TO SHOOT FLOWERS.

2. Why did the creators of this comic book include this part of a panel on page 19? What is the purpose of the purple outline around Mxy?

I'M *MXYZPTLK!* HOLDER OF THE *FIVE KEYS* THAT UNLOCK THE *FIFTY-TWO LAYERS OF HYPER-REALITY!* MY MIND HAS BECOME ONE WITH *ALL TEN POSSIBLE DIMENSIONS!* WHO ARE *YOU* TO CHALLENGE *ME?!*

3. Why do you think Mxy's former friends punished him by making him two-dimensional? Why would that be unpleasant for Mxy?

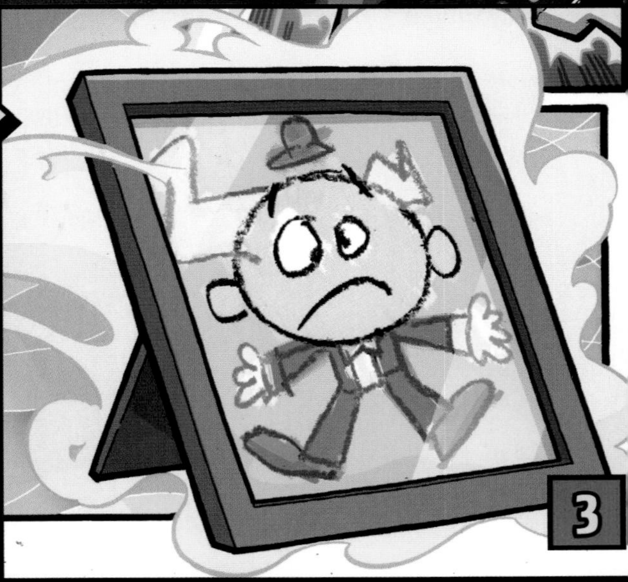
3

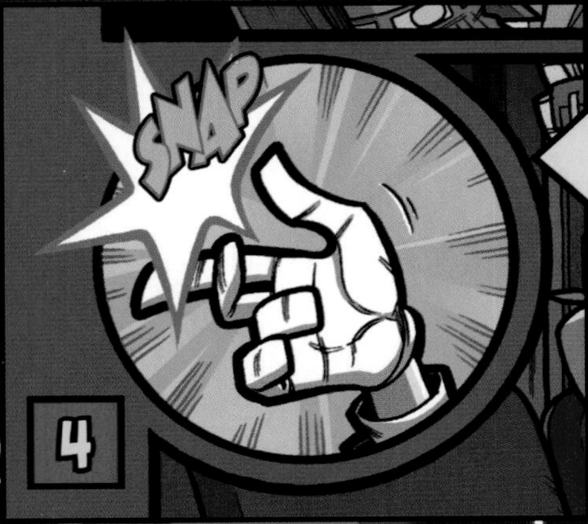
SNAP
4

4. This panel appears on page 10. Why did the creators decide to put this panel where they did? What purpose does it serve?

5. In your own words, explain why some of the speech bubbles in this panel [and the surrounding ones] are lighter than the others.

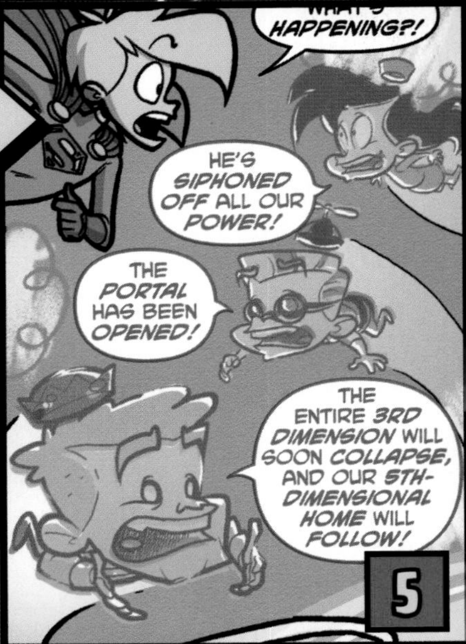
HAPPENING?!
HE'S SIPHONED OFF ALL OUR POWER!
THE PORTAL HAS BEEN OPENED!
THE ENTIRE 3RD DIMENSION WILL SOON COLLAPSE, AND OUR 5TH-DIMENSIONAL HOME WILL FOLLOW!
5

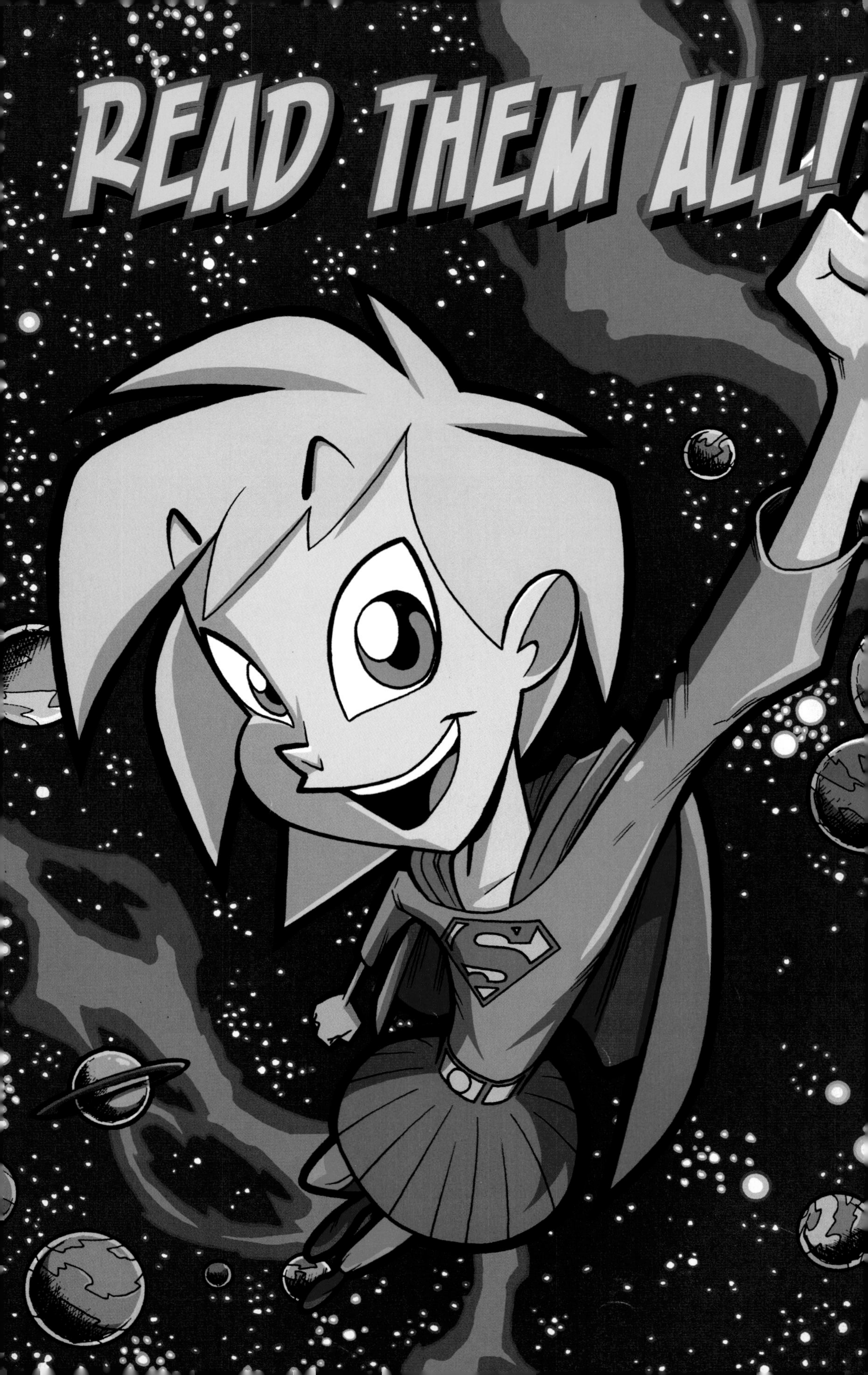
READ THEM ALL!

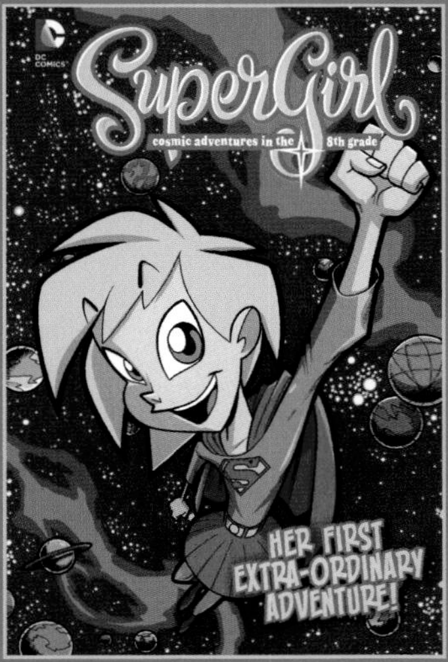
DC COMICS
SuperGirl
cosmic adventures in the 8th grade
HER FIRST EXTRA-ORDINARY ADVENTURE!

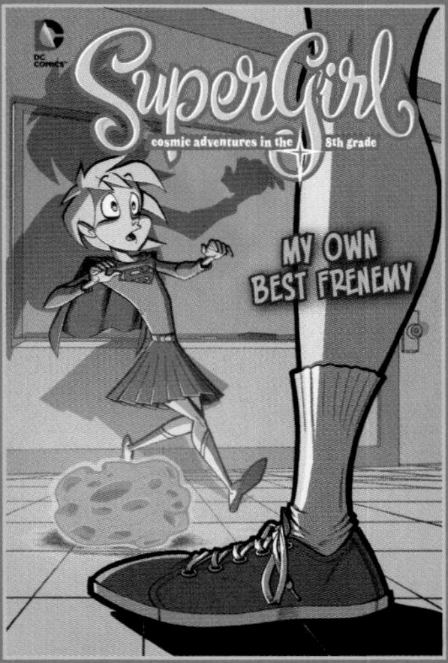
DC COMICS
SuperGirl
cosmic adventures in the 8th grade
MY OWN BEST FRENEMY

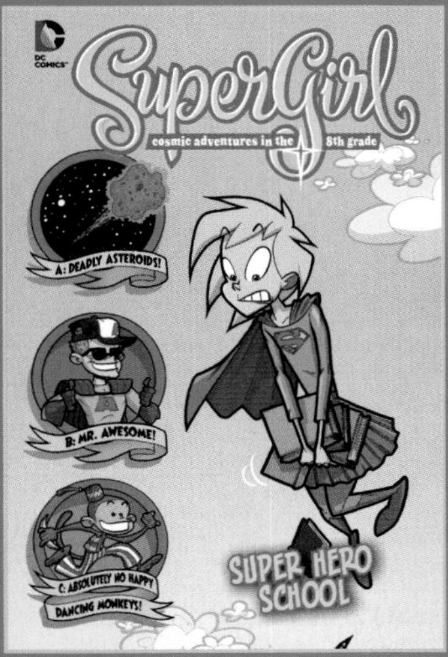
DC COMICS
SuperGirl
cosmic adventures in the 8th grade
A: DEADLY ASTEROIDS!
B: MR. AWESOME!
C: ABSOLUTELY NO HAPPY DANCING MONKEYS!
SUPER HERO SCHOOL

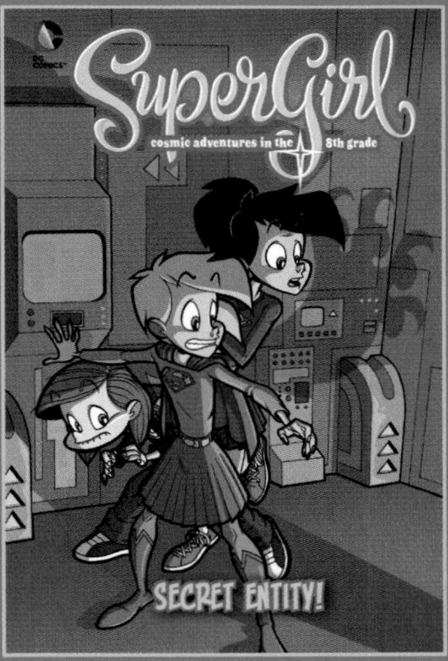
DC COMICS
SuperGirl
cosmic adventures in the 8th grade
SECRET ENTITY!

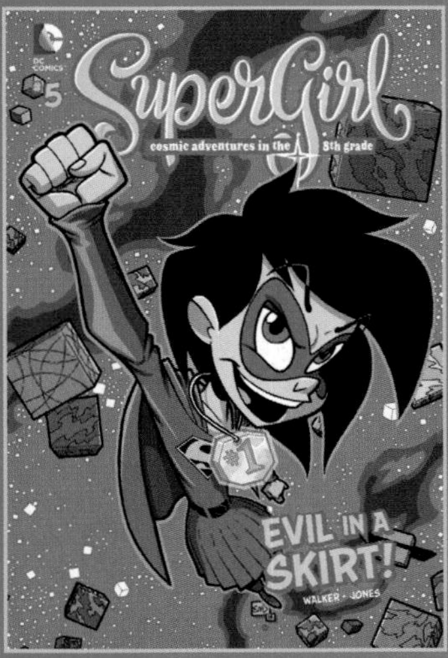
DC COMICS
5
SuperGirl
cosmic adventures in the 8th grade
EVIL IN A SKIRT!
WALKER • JONES

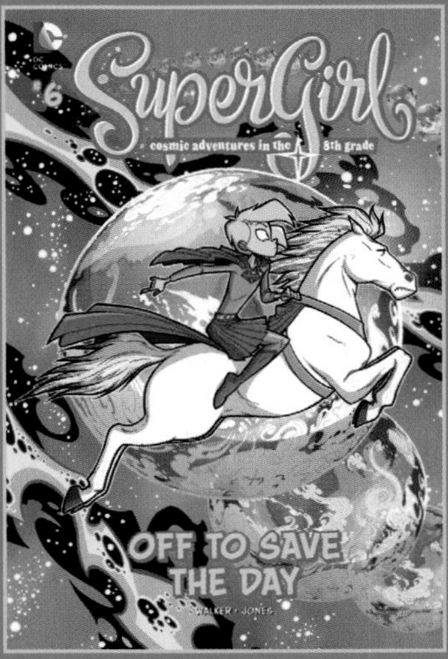
6
SuperGirl
cosmic adventures in the 8th grade
OFF TO SAVE THE DAY
WALKER • JONES

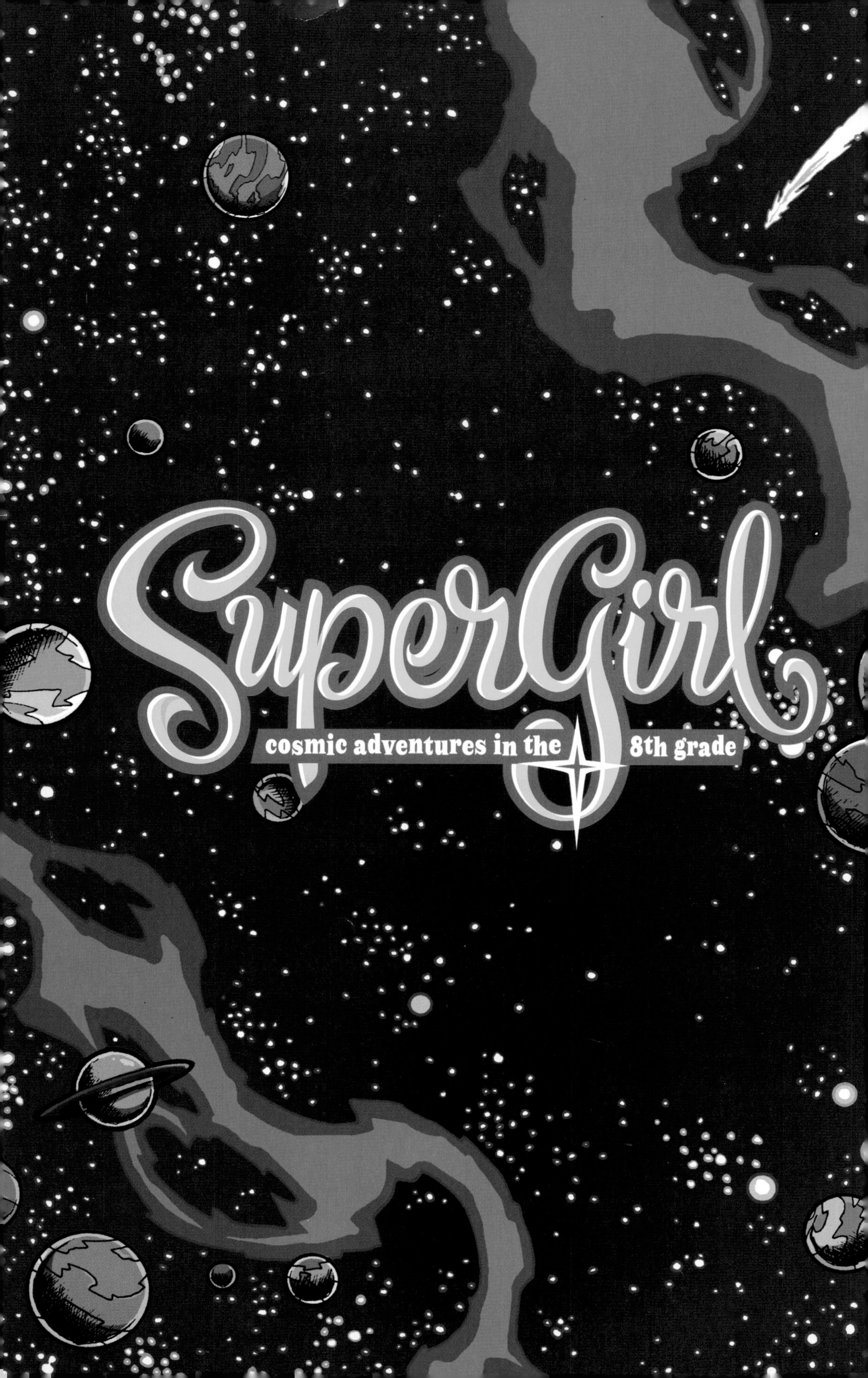
SuperGirl
cosmic adventures in the 8th grade